Dr. Cue

ERIC
CORBYN

TAG Publishing, LLC
2030 S. Milam
Amarillo, TX 79109
www.TAGPublishers.com
info@TAGPublishers.com

ISBN: 978-1-599304410

First Edition

Cover Art by Andy Chase Cundiff

Dr. Cue

ERIC CORBYN

Author's Note

Eric Corbyn, the author of this book, wrote nearly 85% of it almost 50 years ago. He was inspired by the work of Ian Felming and read all of the James Bond novels. He was also inspired by the motion pictures, *From Russia with Love* and *Goldfinger.*

Eric decided to write his own spy novel along those same lines emulating the work of Ian Fleming's novels and completed this text in the spring of 2015.

CHAPTER ONE

The soft rays of the sun beamed through the cloud openings below, slowly giving way to the inevitable encroachment of nightfall. On this April evening in the spring of '88 the sun made its final appearance and slowly sank into the distant sea. Like a lighthouse beacon gasping out its final beam, the rays skimmed along the ocean top, rolling out a red carpet toward the shoreline ahead. Not far away, high tide waves could be heard as they slapped and pulled at the impenetrable cliffs along the Jamaican coast. Above these cliffs, a small object crossed the path of this narrow red beam and moved quietly along the coastal road that paralleled the ocean for several miles. The driver of the car, Preston James, followed the winding road far into the night until finally the road forked. The left road led to an ocean-front house that had been reserved for the weekend by Tanya Ray, the attractive blonde who rode next to Preston. Soon, the moonlit circular house appeared high on a cliff overlooking the sea, as if a spaceship had landed on the bluff.

Two hours later, after a quiet dinner on the terrace, the couple retired for the night, finally resting in their shared waterbed. As always, Preston placed his Beretta under his pillow, turned to Tanya, and kissed her softly on the lips. "Tomorrow we won't be so tired. We'll have an interesting day in town and an evening to remember, I promise you."

"Good night, Preston." Tanya returned his kiss and closed her eyes. Before long, her breathing indicated she was fast asleep. Preston took one last drag of his cigarette, his mind making its final thoughts of the day before going to sleep. *A very contemporary house*, Preston observed. It was exceptionally decorated by a friend of Tanya's, a renowned interior designer and the owner of the house. The house itself was a complete circle that rotated on an axis, making one full turn every hour. The outside was surrounded by large windows, and the building gave the impression of a huge flattened toy top that had been dropped into the rocky craters.

The round house contained several unusually shaped rooms, each cleverly decorated in its own unique style. The pride of the house was the comfortably large bedroom: one end contained a large bathroom with a sauna and a glassed-in shower with gold-plated fixtures; the other end had an oversized black marble bathtub with strong water jets, located next to a large, curved window. The woman who occasionally shared this bathing experience was careful to time her bath to correspond to the house's rotation, in order to enjoy the view of the ocean. Particularly at night, she could relax her tired muscles, feel the powerful jets of water massage her body, sip champagne by candlelight, and admire the starlit ocean waters. She might even catch a brightly lit ocean liner moving effortlessly across the dark green waters of the distant horizon.

Next to the bathroom were a dressing area and a large sitting area, which contained a large L-shaped white couch, chairs, and tables of unusual shapes and sizes. The waterbed was located in a "hayloft," a cubbyhole accessible only by a small oak stairway. A horseshoe-shaped window, its base the same height as the bed, encircled this petite chamber. These windows reached upwards almost ten feet and gave the occupants of this bungalow a spectacular view of the sea and surrounding landscape. The owner of this house had gone to great lengths to make the surroundings appear to thrust into the room like objects darting from an old 3-D movie screen.

Preston had been here only a few short hours, but he could already sense the house's involvement with its natural surroundings. A terrarium behind the waterbed consisted of green plants and a pump that recirculated a small stream of water, trickling around the surrounding vegetation. This sound was relaxing when the windows were closed, as they were now; it was nature's music to sleep by.

The light from the moon shone through this small jungle of plants: occasionally those in bed would let their imaginations run wild. Tonight, however, the terrarium was the farthest thing from Preston's mind, whose thoughts were focused instead on the large antique fan that hovered directly over his head. Preston watched the dark metal blades spin softly in a hypnotic rhythm. Preston closed his eyes. Sensing something was not right, he opened them again and stared at the fan.

"Too large," Preston decided. "Too damn large."

It didn't fit. Here was a house so professionally decorated, so carefully put together—why such a large fan in such a small hayloft area? It didn't make sense. If a breeze was needed, the windows could always be opened. Perhaps a small ceiling fan might make a nice effect, but why such a large and awkward-looking one?

Preston closed his eyes again. *What's the matter with me, making such a fuss over a fan? Go to sleep.* After pulling the single white sheet over his shoulders, he did just that.

Two hours later, at midnight, the large ceiling fan stopped its rotation. The metal blades dipped into a vertical position. The fan, reversing its direction, rotated counter-clockwise at a slower speed than before. At the same time, it descended gradually. Minutes later it had closed two-thirds of the distance between the bed and the ceiling. Now the fan's rotation steadily increased, as it continued downward.

Preston grew more restless in his sleep. He felt the draft on his face. Too tired to open his eyes, he lay in a semi-sleep, wondering where the breeze was coming from. It probably came from a window Tanya had opened, he rationalized. Lying on his left side, he opened his eyes. To his surprise, Tanya was no longer beside him. Even in a drowsy semi-sleep, Preston's instinct, finely tuned as result of twenty years of surviving the espionage games, revealed what he had sensed earlier: TROUBLE. Without a moment's hesitation, he grabbed the Beretta from under his pillow with his left hand and jerked suddenly upward. He raised his head, then abruptly dropped it back.

But it was too late; Preston failed to avoid the sharp rotating blades. One of them slapped sharply across the right side of his forehead, and Preston fell back onto the pillow. Fighting to remain conscious, he lay stunned and partially paralyzed. He tried to scoot sideways, but couldn't. He tried again, but again could not move his body. It was an eerie sensation, as if he'd been in a deep freeze.

He had only felt so immobile once before. Years ago, he'd come to on an operation table. He could hear the doctors talking over him, and he could feel a tube being pushed down his throat. He heard a nurse in the background warn that his blood pressure was dangerously high. Yet he couldn't open his eyes or tell them that he was awake. It was awful. He was experiencing the same frightening helpless sensation now.

Preston looked straight above; the fan was now less than two feet from his face and continued its downward spin. The noise from the rotation now reached such a strong hum that it gave Preston the chilling feeling he was about to be slaughtered by an old DC-3 propeller. In hopeless disgust, his gun lying useless in his hand, Preston fired. The first shot shattered the window. His arm moved back toward his left side. Jerking and quivering, he managed to pull off four more shots. His finger was barely able to fire the fifth, and was too weak to fire a sixth.

The bullets fired at an angle and ripped through the plastic waterbed not far from his legs. One riffled through the top cover like a pebble skipping through a pond. Water spewed everywhere. The weight from the flowing water shredded the waterbed's base. Like a small waterfall, the flow trickled down the stairway. In the meantime, Preston lay in a hopeless daze, feeling paralyzed, frustrated, and— worst of all, according to his standards—stupid. The fan, now less than a foot from his face, continued its descent as the strong wind blew Preston's hair violently and rippled the water like ocean waves.

The blood spurted from his wound, covering his face and staining the pillow and the sheet below him. The wind from the lowering fan, now so strong and close to Preston's face, scattered the blood like large fresh raindrops. Preston lay without moving, barely conscious. It had seemed an eternity, but in reality all this happened in less than fifty seconds. In those final few seconds, after Preston had fired his last bullet, countless thoughts raced across Preston's mind. Incidents of his life flashed before his blood-soaked eye. He recalled careless mistakes he'd made. He guessed that he'd been drugged by Tanya, and he wondered why. She was so insistent on their having an after-dinner drink; now he knew why. He cursed himself again for beings careless, for not following his instincts.

"Another goddamn rat caught in a trap," he mumbled to himself. "Bitch! You lousy bitch!" Preston screamed out in agony—in actuality, an inaudible whisper. "You've really done it to yourself this time." With this final thought, Preston lay on his blood-soaked pillow, his semiconscious thoughts now giving way to a conscious one: the dark, hovering executioner now within inches of his face. Its speed had reached such an intensity that the long bar that connected the fan to the ceiling began to vibrate violently as it continued its final descent, like a shark stalking its wounded prey, toward the bloody lifeless face below.

Preston, near death from loss of blood, faded into unconsciousness, no longer aware of his dilemma. At the base of the bed, the flow of blood streamed out like water from holes in a dyke. The bluish-green flow changed to an ominous orange-red as it gushed down the stairway, as if trying to escape the massacre about to occur only seconds away

Dr. Cue

CHAPTER TWO

Twenty nine days later in the largest hospital in Kingston, Jamaica, a tall, lanky man in a gray suit waited impatiently, flipping a coin in his hand. This nervous gesture continued for more than thirty minutes, until a heavyset black nurse approached the man.

"You can come in now, but only for a short time." The tall man followed the burly nurse out of the waiting room and down the hall to the second room on the left. "He's still in critical condition. We don't want to risk losing him to a coma again," she warned. "So make it quick, and don't excite him."

"I won't be but a moment," the man promised in his deep English accent. He proceeded into the room, pulling a nearby chair up next to the bed. He watched Preston for a minute, observing his heavily bandaged head, noting that his face was so pale that it was hard to distinguish it from the bandages.

Preston, his eyes closed, his face motionless, mumbled: "Good morning, Roger." Opening his eyes, he rose up on his pillows and extended his hand. "It's totally out of the question. I am not going to cover for you this weekend. So you can forget it. Don't even bother to ask me." Preston managed a weak smile. "But how about a cigarette?"

Roger, a friend since their British secret service days, shook his head in disbelief.

"You never change, do you Preston? That's all you need—a cigarette. That nurse told me you were in serious condition."

"They're prone to exaggeration. Actually I couldn't feel better. Don't worry. I'm going to be out of this zoo in no time. It's depressing around here, and the bartenders are lousy." Roger lit a cigarette, took a drag, and placed it in Preston's mouth. "That nurse will kick my ass if she catches you."

"You could have at least brought me a scotch." Preston inhaled deeply and slowly blew the smoke out, savoring his first cigarette in nearly a month.

"By the way, I'm thinking of getting out of this illustrious profession. I've always admired Gandhi. Might even retire to India." Preston paused for a moment, his eyes growing more serious. "It's great to be alive. How the hell did I get out of this one, Roger? Or is this not real? Am I in a dream somewhere?"

Roger scooted his chair closer to Preston and began his revelation. "For starters, Preston, as you have no doubt realized, that girl set you up. You were drugged, just enough to immobilize you. But she was careful not to knock you out." Roger turned his chair around and leaned his arms on the back. "You pissed 'em off this time. They really went out of their way to get even with you."

"Why the hell didn't they just kill me after I was drugged? Even that bitch Tanya could have done away with me."

"Preston, Tanya was arrested at the airport the next day, by your agents. During an extensive interrogation, she broke down and spilled the beans. Seems that last April, on assignment in Istanbul, you killed her GB lover. Tanya believed you murdered him in cold blood"

"*That's not true!*" Preston snapped.

"Well . . . it doesn't matter now. Tanya is in London. She almost pulled it off: Preston James, secret agent, gets chopped to pieces by an old ceiling fan while passed out in a waterbed." Roger smiled and clapped his hands, "Boy, wouldn't that make front page headlines in every tabloid in Europe? Nice little scandal, don't you think?"

"Why didn't it happen, Roger?"

"Count your blessings from now on, Preston, "Roger lectured, "Every break that could have possibly gone your way, did. The smartest thing you ever did was fire those shots. You emptied the waterbed just enough to lower your body from the fan's blades: break number one. Also, the loss of the water caused the left side of the bed to collapse. You rolled over, resting on your right side, which helped slow the bleeding and kept you out of the path of the fan: break number two. The waterbed continued to leak, which saved you from a good electrocution: break number three."

Preston put out his cigarette and motioned Roger for another one. Roger handed a smoke to Preston, who sat upright on the bed.

"Go on."

"The glass from the window you shot shattered into several pieces. Some of the glass hit two small greenhouses below: break number four. At the same time, the bedroom had rotated away from the ocean and faced the road. A security guard heading to work at a house down the way heard the commotion and investigated. Even low tide helped; the guard might not have heard the noise if it weren't such a still night. He entered the front door, left ajar by your fleeing friend. He told me that when he saw you there, the fan was less than three inches from the bed. Three more inches, and you would have been fried. The guard stopped the bleeding with ice and was able to get you to the small hospital in the nearby town. You were a pint of blood away from being history. How you made it, no one knows. Twenty-five days in a coma. Thirty-one stitches, a nice little brain concussion."

"It must be my clean living," Preston said.

"Anyhow, they transferred you to this hospital several weeks ago. But it's not over yet. You have a long way to go." Roger took the cigarette out of Preston's hand and extinguished it. "Come to think of it, I'm nuts for giving you these." Roger shook his head and continued. "It's not like it used to be, Preston. When we were young. The healing doesn't come easy anymore. As soon as you're able, you are going to London for an extended period."

Roger stood up, stretched, and backhanded Preston softly on his arm. "Get some rest. I'll see you again tomorrow. I better get out of here before the Gestapo comes in." Roger headed for the door, giving Preston a farewell salute. "And one other thing: you owe me one. I've been covering assignments for the both of us."

"Thanks, Roger I'll make it up to you. Hopefully I'll join you in London soon."

Dr. Cue

CHAPTER THREE

"Have a seat, Preston. The colonel will be with you in a moment. You're a bit early." The woman behind the desk was dressed in a charcoal gray business suit with a white ruffled blouse. Danielle was in her early forties, barely five feet tall with a good figure, quite attractive, beautiful facial features, light brown hair, and deep blue eyes. Preston sat down in the hunter-green wingback chair by a large window not far from her desk.

"And how are you doing this fine spring morning, Danielle?" Preston asked.

"Good morning." Danielle smiled. "Hope you rested up in London. I'm sorry about your unfortunate accident in Jamaica. For a while, we didn't think you were going to make it." Danielle couldn't help but throw that in. After all, this was the famous agent Preston James. Slipups rarely came from his direction.

Preston smiled back at her. "Oh, yes, good ol' Jamaica. I've always been a fan of hers. Indeed, it's nice to be back in action again after a long layoff."

Danielle gathered a few folders, turned to Preston, and pointed to the table next to him. "There's mineral water and coffee; help yourself. I'll be back shortly."

Preston poured a drink from the large mineral bottle. Musing to himself, he asked, "What ever happened to the royal treatment? How times have changed. Well, anyway, it was fun while it lasted." Preston continued his admiration for Danielle; who would have believed, when she was the newest agent to join their organization that she'd prove to be one of the best.

Preston leaned back, lit a cigarette—his third of the day—and gazed through the window beside him, watching the boats go up and down the Seine. "Such a spectacle of action and beauty," he mused. "Such a thriving city. No wonder so much had been written about it. Day and night, so much going on—such incredible food, such magnificent buildings and gardens."

Preston took another deep drag from his cigarette and reminisced about the first time he arrived here, years ago for a brief weekend. He had visited every major attraction: Notre Dame; the majestic Sacre Couer, built on a hill overlooking the city; the Arc de Triomphe, designed by Napoleon in honor of his victorious army. But the Eiffel tower was his favorite. Such an eyesore to Parisians at first, it had since become one of Europe's most famous attractions. No wonder Paris is considered the most romantic city in the world, Preston thought. There's nothing more awesome than to look across a city of ten million people at night from the highest observation deck on the Eiffel tower, to see these incredible sights lit up like thousands of Christmas trees. The buildings didn't seem real; they looked more like brightly lit porcelain figures in a shop window.

"To hell with the sights!" Preston changed his line of thought. The best thing about Paris was their women— so feminine, so natural, and so sensuous. They were totally different from the women of any other country in Europe. That was fascination of Europe; you can cross a border and enter into an all-new culture. Take the German women, for example: they seemed so rigid, so serious, and so disciplined—the opposite of the French women. Preston leaned forward and put out his cigarette. He stood up by the window and mumbled: "I think I'll just have to retire here someday."

Preston was a good-looking man of forty-six, slightly gray in the temples with a definite receding hairline. He had sharp facial features, well-defined with a square jaw. Hard lines appeared on his face, brought about by the wear and tear of his profession. His brown eyes projected intelligence and character. When they wanted to they could stare holes through you, but for the most part there was a spark of kindness to them. Preston stood just a shade less than six feet tall. He was in good physical condition for his age, and he could still wear a forty-two long custom suit with only one change through the years: a fluctuating waist line that fell somewhere between thirty-four and thirty-five inches. He refused to let his tailor cut the extra inch; vanity made Preston wear his trousers—always pleated—slightly lower during these times. However, in his business one did not allow oneself to become complacent. There was too much at stake. Those who did didn't last long. Keeping physically fit was mandatory.

Preston had been with the British Secret Service for seventeen years before his "retirement" four years ago. After a year of forced inactivity, which was not to his liking, he accepted his new position as agent 44 of the International Secret Service. This newly formed organization consisted of twenty agents: two from the USA, two from Great Britain, two from Germany, two from France, and two from Italy, plus ten back-up agents.

The organization's ostensible purpose was to track down stolen art objects and return them to the museums from which they were stolen. They still did this occasionally, to maintain their cover. The ISS had two headquarters; one was in Paris, not far from the Louvre, overlooking the Seine.

The other was located in London, not far from 10 Downing Street. The real purpose of the ISS was to fight international terrorism. The ISS was headed by a retired British Secret Service commander, Winston Randolph, commonly referred to as "the Colonel."

Their activities and missions were of the utmost secrecy. Even the ISS's lone secretary, Danielle Foquet, was an agent. During their meetings, no records were kept. In case of a break in, it was Danielle's job to write falsified minutes about art thefts and related discussions.

Preston had always felt the great show of secrecy was a bit overplayed, but then, he knew why it was necessary. After all, it seemed that too many covert operations in the past had been exposed or leaked. It was happening more and more often in recent years.

During his own British Secret Service career, a licensed-to-kill agent had been arrested as a double agent. His cocaine addiction had been too much for him—a disgrace to the agency. "The world is changing," Preston noted to himself. It seemed that there was little honor left among people anymore. Maybe it was the new generation trying to keep up with everybody. Such a selfish lot.

That's what Preston most admired about the Colonel. He was a man of honor and integrity. Now sixty three years of age, he was in splendid condition. His appearance always reminded Preston of what Winston Churchill would have looked like had he been a heavyweight boxer all his life. Winston was six feet tall and solid as a brick wall. He was the classic leader; a more perfect stereotype of his position could not be found. He was mostly bald, round faced, double chinned, with ears larger than he cared to have. A man of much discipline and self-control, he rarely drank—only an occasional glass of red wine with a special dinner. His only indulgence was the constant presence of a hand-rolled cigar.

The Colonel's credentials were endless. His English mother had married his American father, and they'd lived in the US from the time Winston was fourteen. He was a graduate of West Point and reached the rank of colonel before his retirement at the age of forty-eight. Winston returned to England, entered the British Secret Service, and became its head in his twelfth year of service. His amazingly quick advancement reflected his remarkable accomplishments within the service. Winston had retired four years ago, disgusted with too much politicking and what he called "softies in the business." He left to form the ISS, an organization he could run the way he wanted with little outside interference.

He decided on ten primary agents and ten back-up agents—and no more. He handpicked the finest agents in their field, and his desire for the utmost secrecy border lined on the absurd, but everyone in the department knew his reasons: Winston's only son had been blown to bits four years ago on assignment in Austria, the result of a double agent exposing him. The double agent was later revealed and prosecuted, but how many more were there?

Winston vowed that this would never happen again under his supervision. Thus, he conceived the ISS. "Hell, if I can't trust twenty of the finest handpicked agents in the world, then the Western world is too decedent to stay free and it deserves what it gets." Winston said. "If anyone ever betrays me," he added, "I'll put a bullet right through his forehead—legal or not."

A broad smile crossed Preston's face as he pictured Winston trotting out these comments, as he did over and over again. Preston looked down at his British Khaki watch: 12:05. "Time for another cigarette. I wonder what's taking the Colonel so long." The Colonel was a stickler for punctuality. Suddenly the door opened and the Colonel entered, walking toward his office with hardly a glance at Preston.

"I see you're still inhaling those damn cigarettes, Preston. One of these days it's going to catch up with you," the Colonel blurted as Preston followed him into his office. "Damn traffic jam tied me up for thirty minutes. Hell, next time I'll just walk." Winston sat down behind his desk and relit his cigar while looking Preston up and down, noting his finely tailored glen plaid suit, pleated trousers, green pencil-striped pinpoint oxford straight collared shirt, and multi-colored paisley tie. The tan Polo tassel loafers bothered the Colonel more than anything; he never approved of Preston's dress and would often chide him about it. Leaning back in his chair, Winston began his lecture. "Three months out of service, James. All the result of your thinking with the little head instead of the big one."

"Yes, you might say that I fanned that assignment," Preston sarcastically replied.

"Your witticisms do not impress me. The next time a stupid incident like that occurs, you can consider yourself on permanent leave," Winston growled. "You're the finest agent I've ever come across. You have only one major weakness: you're a sucker for women. One of these days you'll learn the hard way." The Colonel rose from his chair, walked over to a slide projector, took several slides out of his briefcase, and began to set up the projector.

"Please turn out the overhead light and have a seat," the Colonel ordered. "Your next assignment is now beginning." The first slide on the wall appeared. The heavy-set figure of a man with a Fu Manchu beard and mustache appeared. He was about five feet eight inches and weighed somewhere around 230 pounds, Preston guessed.

"Preston, this is Dr. Sebastian Cue. You might have heard the name before. He's the eighth ranked pool player in the world. His real name is Sebastian Belcheff, and he was born in Bulgaria sixty-one years ago." The Colonel continued with different slides showing Dr. Cue in several different poses, including several shots from a pool tournament. "At the age of twenty-eight, he received his medical degree. He immigrated to the US in 1965 and practiced medicine for sixteen years, quitting in 1981 as the result of his fascination with pool. The CIA has long suspected him of espionage activities, but they could never prove anything. He's one of the craftiest men you'll ever meet—a genius. His IQ, according to old medical files we found, has been rated at just over 190. He's a total ego freak and a megalomaniac. He's quite the celebrity; Las Vegas loves him. He's constantly mixing with entertainers and movie stars. He is entertaining, charming, and intellectual- a personality that can charm almost anyone. Seven years ago, Dr. Cue moved from Las Vegas to a small castle on the German-Swiss border in the Bavarian Alps. The castle is referred to as 'The Fortress.'" The Colonel showed several pictures of the castle, shot from different angles. "It's definitely a fortress. Heavily guarded, with a security system second to none and Dobermans everywhere. He even had a moat built around it, as you can see in the next picture. Dr. Cue lives here. However, for the past two years he's been traveling extensively—one trip a week on the Concord to the states, primarily ending up in Las Vegas. Also, numerous trips to Venice, where he'll stay up to three days at a time.

"His brother, Bela Belcheff, was arrested in Switzerland recently, and is now serving a twenty-year term for heroin smuggling. We've proven that he is indeed Dr. Cue's brother, even though they were separated at a very early age. His brother lived with his father in Venice, and very few people are aware of their kinship. Bela has long been suspected by Swiss intelligence of international terrorism, and he's been responsible for several bombings in France and Germany, though no evidence has been gathered to prove these allegations. His terrorist activities were bankrolled by his drug activities. We've long suspected that he is also a covert member of the KGB. We have uncovered countless trips make by Bela to the Soviet Union from the late seventies up until a year ago. He has lived in Venice since 1977 and owns a small antique shop as his cover.

"Their father was a very successful business man who became wealthy thanks to his success in the jewelry business—until his American investments were wiped out by the Depression. He filed for bankruptcy and was never the same. His bitter feelings toward the US and capitalism became an obsession that both his sons adopted. Their father resorted to farming, eventually living in Venice. His health has deteriorated in recent years."

The Colonel rose stretched, puffed heavily on his cigar, and turned to Preston: "So you're sitting there wondering what in the hell does all this mean, right?" Before Preston could answer, the Colonel continued, "Well, we don't know what to think; we're totally at loss. But we know something is up. We have received indirect reports from our various sources that Cue is still into espionage activities. We have also been led to believe that he's planning for his brother's escape from the Swiss prison. How, we don't know. The SOB is a clever rascal. Hell, he's even more secretive in his actions than I am. But sooner or later we're going to burst his bubble, you can count on that. And now Preston, for the fun and games." The Colonel handed over a small piece of paper containing several code words. Preston slowly opened it. The following phrases appeared:

PHYSICAL FITNESS

CHAMPIONSHIP POOL

VENICE

SANTA FE SAM, "THE SHARK"

The last phrase amused Preston. Who the hell was Santa Fe Sam, "The Shark?" But the words that really shook him were the dreaded "physical fitness." Every year, agents had to attend six weeks of intensive training, alternating summer one year and winter the next. Last winter Preston spent six weeks practicing skiing techniques, hang gliding, fencing, and repelling. Some of the training seemed outlandish, but it was the Colonel's feeling that as each year passed the opposition was growing harder to compete with.

To combat the skills of the enemy, the Colonel had begun "basic training" for his agents three years ago in attempt to gain superiority. Every year it was different, from toboggan-riding to polo, from riding the rapids in Colorado to mountain climbing in the Alps—the list went on and on. One never knew what to expect. The damndest of them all to Preston had been learning to ride camels during a summer training course in Morocco.

"Physical fitness" was the Colonel's way of letting him know that he wasn't in as good a shape as he should be. It would be rough, but he'd gone through it several times before. The Colonel took the slides from the projector and began running them through the shredding machine. They would be burned later. Preston gazed at the piece of paper. Before each assignment, code words were given to each agent.

"Well, Preston, do I have your undivided attention now?" the Colonel asked.

"Yes, you do sir. But . . . the Santa Fe Shark?"

The Colonel chuckled for a moment. "This is your assignment. Tomorrow you'll fly to Las Vegas, where you will spend six weeks in basic training. You'll receive extensive lessons in pool from one of the best in the business. One of the reasons you were chosen for this assignment was because of your excellent pool playing during your service in the Royal Navy. Although you're no doubt on the rusty side. We figure that with a little brush-up work and a bit of mechanical imagination from our engineers, you'll be able to look somewhat professional. We're going to set up a little action with Dr. Cue.

"He has one major weakness; he is a compulsive gambler. But unlike most compulsive gamblers, he wins more than he loses. After your training, we're going to set you up with a high-dollar pool match with him at his castle.

The only way we could figure out how to do this was for you to play the part of the Santa Fe Shark, generally known as Santa Fe Sam. I'll give you a brief history about this man: He was the tenth-rated pool player in the world, but eight years ago during a gas explosion at a plant where he was working, half of his face was badly scarred and burned. From that date on, he has refused any public appearances. He shuns Las Vegas, does not allow any pictures to be taken of himself. But he still plays pool constantly, mostly in private homes. He plays in limited tournaments, on the condition that there will be no spectators or cameras. Why he won't undergo plastic surgery is a mystery to everyone.

"Anyway, after basic training is over, we intend to set up a match with Dr. Cue for you. With a little help from our makeup department you'll fit just fine in the role. You will be vacationing in Europe this summer, and will challenge the Doc to a bit of sporting action at his place. He'll jump at the opportunity. Hopefully you can stay there long enough to do a little snooping—he rarely allows visitors to his place. There are two parts to the castle; the back section where he spends a lot of his time is off limits. Nobody is allowed back there except for a few trusted aides, and hopefully in the near future, a nice little chap from Santa Fe, New Mexico. That's all for now, Preston. You will report to Las Vegas on Monday, where one of our agents will meet you at the airport. I suggest you enjoy the weekend ahead, for you've got a lot of work ahead of you. Good day, Preston. I will see you in seven weeks."

Dr. Cue

32

CHAPTER FOUR

Strolling along, Preston looked at his watch. "Damn, it's already 5:30. Saturday is almost over with," Preston griped. "Weekends go too fast." He wasn't looking forward to his six weeks of training in Vegas. He couldn't keep it off his mind.

Preston gave himself a pep talk: "Here you are on the action-packed Champ Elysees in the heart of Paris. Enjoy yourself." He continued down the avenue to the familiar sight of the Arc de Triomphe, towering above. "How many times have I seen those old newsreels that showed victorious armies marching under this archway?" Preston reflected. In particular, he remembered Hitler's arrogant march, signaling the beginning of the Nazi occupation of Paris. But the most memorable newsreel that Preston remembered was the boisterous celebration when the Allies reclaimed France from the Nazis and celebrated by parading their soldiers and tanks down this broad avenue. There wasn't a city in the world like Paris—so beautiful, so imperialistic, so bright, so much gaiety, so much happening. There was never a quiet moment in this incredible city. *Action! Action! Action!* The city was not for the meek that was for sure. This, without question, was the most romantic city in the world.

At night, the center of the city was the biggest, brightest midway anywhere in the world. 365 days of the year, lights sparkled, champagne corks popped, music filled the air, and couples embraced in romance.

Preston continued his stroll down the avenue, lighting up a cigarette as he observed the most exclusive clothing shops in Paris. Paris was the crossroads of the world. Every nationality imaginable paraded up and down the avenue as though they were on their way to a never-ending costume ball. There were Arabs in their chic garb, lanky black Africans in animal skin prints and unusual hats, Chinese so recognizable in their rigid clothing, fast-moving Japanese, stern-faced Russians. But the most amusing citizens to frequent this avenue were the silly American tourists, who attracted more stares from the locals than anyone else. Parisians did not approve of the shorts that so many of the American tourists wore in the summer. To Parisians, this was not acceptable; only women were allowed this privilege.

Red-faced American tourists, no matter how wealthy or powerful they might be, were turned away by the finest cafes as a result of their inappropriate dress.

Preston crossed the wide avenue, dodging cars and headed for Le Fouquet's Paris—the most renown of all outdoor cafes on the Champ Elysées. He approached one of the outdoor tables, but his attention was focused on a woman who had walked in just ahead of him. She seated herself at one of the tables not far from the avenue. Preston stopped by the curb, lit a cigarette, and observed her with interest.

There was something mysterious about this woman, but he didn't know what it was. Maybe it was the way she sauntered across the avenue, or maybe it was the way she tucked her long, dark hair behind her right ear. Whatever it was, Preston sensed something out of the ordinary about her, and this intrigued him. Preston continued to observe her, admiring her silk paisley dress, bright in color, the hem falling slightly above her knees and revealing perfectly shaped legs. She had pitch-black hair, wide lips, high cheek bones, and beautiful blue eyes. This was a woman of much elegance and sophistication, Preston surmised.

The woman turned sideways, apparently annoyed by Preston's constant stares. By now, it was just too good for Preston to pass up. "She's probably married," Preston reasoned. "But what the hell, it's worth a try." Preston approached her table, "Good afternoon," Preston offered, "A glass of Dom Pérignon would be a nice way to enjoy the lovely afternoon."

"I'd rather you didn't—"

Before the lady could finish, Preston pulled up a chair beside her and interrupted: "Thank you." He spoke hastily and motioned to the waiter. "Garçon, please bring the nice lady and I a bottle of Dom Pérignon'79." Turning to the woman, Preston inquired, "My name is Preston James. And your name is . . . ?"

"Not for you to know, Mr. James." She was obviously a bit irritated by Preston's advances. "I don't think you listen well. I did not request your company. Rudeness is not well received in this city, Mr. James. I suggest you brush up on your manners." The lady continued to stare at Preston, obviously uncomfortable with his presence.

Preston, encouraged somewhat after noticing that she was not wearing a wedding ring, was determined to try again. In a low soft voice, he attempted to console her. "I do apologize for my abruptness, but shall we say that your beauty and elegance completely overwhelmed me."

"Apparently, you are not listening," the lady replied. "You are not welcome. Please go away."

Preston knew he was losing control of the encounter. Unless he could come up with something fast, his chances to be with her would soon end. "Please be at ease. It's a beautiful Saturday afternoon on the Champ Elysees. Allow me the honor of sharing a glass of champagne with you and I'll be on my merry way. I can assure you, I don't bite."

The woman studied Preston for a moment. She tapped her right foot in a nervous gesture and offered no immediate response. Her face showed no emotion. Preston waited patiently, remembering the old sales rule: *He who speaks first, loses.* Preston remained silent. Finally, she managed a weak smile.

"I didn't intend to be so brusque with you, Mr. James," she explained. "It's not you. There are other reasons for my not wishing your company."

"Is it another man?" Preston asked.

"No, that's not the reason. I do not wish to discuss it further." The garçon arrived at the table, poured two glasses of champagne, and placed the bottle in an iced container to the right of Preston.

"Shall we toast?" Preston said. "To a very lovely woman in a very romantic city." The lady hesitated but reluctantly raised her glass. After taking a sip, she reached into her purse, pulled out a pair of Porsche sunglasses, and put them on.

"Are you going to tell me your name?" Preston inquired.

"Sabrina, and that's all you need to know."

Preston smiled. The two studied each other for almost a minute without saying a word. Before a new conversation could begin, an unusual street performer approached the table. The café crowd cheered as the freaky-looking performer began to tease the elderly couple next to their table. Street performers like this one were always favorites; there were so many unique acts. These performers were licensed by the city, and the good ones made decent tips walking up and down the busy avenue mocking tourists and doing whatever it took to please their audience.

This particular performer was very tall, six-foot-five or more, and extremely thin. He had a large, protruding nose and ears way too big for his head, and he was dressed in a knee-length black tuxedo and a stovepipe hat. His eyes were covered in dark makeup, but the rest of his face was powdered white. He looked like a walking corpse, or like Abraham Lincoln on heavy drugs.

Preston and Sabrina continued to watch his robotic performance, as he mocked and tormented the elderly couple without saying a word. The delighted patrons laughed, clapping their approval.

"He's the best robot performer I've seen on this avenue." Sabrina scrutinized the weird man. "He must be new. I thought I had seen all of the street performers, but I have never seen him before."

The street performer turned his attention away from the elderly couple and focused on Sabrina. He didn't move at first, cocking his head to the left in a mechanical gesture and remaining motionless. He stared at Sabrina and did not blink—not once. He looked like a mannequin that had been removed from a Halloween store window. He stared directly at Sabrina's lips, his body frozen stiff, and still he did not blink.

At first Sabrina smiled, but now she was showing signs of discomfort. Finally the street performer stiff-legged his way toward them, moving his arms and legs in slow motion like a toy soldier that had been wound up with a key. In a series of jerking motions, he reached his arm forward toward her right hand, his lips extending in hopeful anticipation that she would allow him to kiss her hand. Sabrina refused the gesture and he again reached down, moving two feet closer in his stiff-leg toy soldier motion, begging for her to let him kiss her hand. Sabrina, still shocked by his spooky appearance, laughed but again refused to extend her hand.

The performer slowly raised up and, much to the delight of the crowd that had gathered near the street, lowered his head in the appearance of sadness and rejection. His eyes blinked as if he were about to cry, and he again bent down very slowly and extended his hand toward hers. Tears trickled from his eyes, watering down his makeup. His face begged its final plea for her acceptance. The crown cheered their approval.

Preston smiled. "Go ahead, give the man your hand. He's harmless." Sabrina smiled and reluctantly raised her hand, much to the robot's delight. He answered her gesture with a Cheshire-Cat grin. "Almost sinister," Preston noted, as the street performer knelt forward to kiss her hand. Sabrina felt uncomfortable when his grin gave way to an ominous look.

"Don't, Sabrina!" Preston blurted in a sharp voice. At the same time he reached for the champagne bottle and stood up. He smashed the bottle hard across the performer's extended arm, shattering the glass table below his hand. Blood gushed from the performer's hand, and before the man had time to react Preston smashed the bottle across the side of his head and sent him sprawling backward onto a table before crashing headfirst onto the cement. He lay motionless, unconscious, and possibly dead. Blood gushed from his right ear. The café patrons gasped and looked on in horror.

"Preston, have you gone absolutely mad?" Sabrina blurted in disgust.

"You might say that I've always been the jealous type."

The elderly lady at the next table spoke sharply to Preston: "Young man, what on earth have you done to this poor fellow? He is just a street performer trying to earn a living, have you lost your mind?" Exasperation flushed the lady's face. She walked over to see if the street performer was still alive.

The crowd's restlessness increased. Shouts of anger in various languages were being directed at Preston. Some people even moved toward him, but before they could get at him two French policemen approached and demanded, "How would you like to be arrested for attempted murder?"

Preston hastily lit a cigarette and attempted to explain his actions. "Officers, this man attempted to poison my companion by injecting a needle into her wrist. If you will pull up the performer's right sleeve, you'll notice a spring-loaded poison dart there. It shoots forward very rapidly, penetrating his victim's wrist, and then it is quickly withdrawn back into its holder. This man is not a licensed street performer. He is a hired killer."

The policemen glared at Preston skeptically. Two policemen walked over to the unconscious man, reached down, and pulled up the performer's bloody right sleeve. There, as Preston had attested, was the dart.

"Officers, if you have that liquid analyzed, you'll find that it contains deadly poison." Preston turned his attention around toward Sabrina. "You see, Sabrina, I'm not such a bad . . ." Sabrina was nowhere to be found. She had vanished. "I'll be damned," Preston complained. "Such gratitude. And I doubt I'll ever see her again. How disappointing."

After an hour at the police station, answering question after question, Preston spent the rest of the evening walking up and down the Champs Elysees talking to every waiter, hoping that one knew a beautiful, dark-haired woman named Sabrina. All the information he could gather was pretty much the same, except one garçon remembered her. She could often be seen on weekends, he said. She was always alone, and no one knew much about her. The only clue offered was that the waiter remembered she had once left a Las Vegas MGM lighter behind. Preston gave the man a hefty tip, asking the man to please contact him if he ever saw her again. He gave the waiter a phone number and told him he'd make it worth the man's while.

Later that evening, Preston overlooked the Arc de Triomphe and smoked his final cigarette of the day, reviewing the evening's events. He gazed at the lit-up arteries of Paris below. "Somewhere out there is Sabrina," he whispered. Oh, how he wanted to know where she was. He couldn't erase her from his mind; she was becoming an obsession.

He headed back to the hotel King George the IV for a much-needed night of rest. "What an evening," Preston muttered. "What an evening."

CHAPTER FIVE

The following Monday, Preston arrived in Las Vegas to begin his six weeks of training. During this time, absolutely no foolishness would be accepted from any agent. Every day for nine hard hours, agents would train, learn, and exercise. One could not relax because assignments had to be studied and books read and memorized. The Colonel would not even allow any alcohol to be touched during this period; he felt that it hindered the agent's ability to retain what he was learning.

At least the opportunity to practice pool again would be somewhat interesting; it was a game he'd once excelled at. One of the best teachers in the business would be Preston's coach. "The Splendid Splinter" had been another

Vegas legend for decades. Although he was a year away from turning eighty, he looked good. He'd been nicknamed Splendid Splinter because of his tall, skinny appearance. Some used to tease him, asking him if he'd mind if they used him as a pool cue. He was told that Preston was a wealthy businessman from England and compensated for his services on the condition that he not discuss Preston with anyone.

For six solid weeks, Preston exercised heavily. At night he learned as much as he could about championship pool, reading books going back thirty years. After all, one incorrect answer to Dr. Cue's questions would be an easy giveaway. He also had a brief about Santa Fe Sam 'The Shark'; this document became his bible for the six weeks of training.

"Such a hot dog name," Preston thought. He had to learn everything about the man, his entire biography from day one. Again, he couldn't afford to answer one of Cue's questions incorrectly, and nobody knew what Cue might know about the man. When Preston wasn't studying The Shark, he spent hours reading about Venice. After a while, he knew every major land mark, every major building, every plaza, and every canal by name.

During the day, after completing his morning exercise, Preston spent hours at the pool table being coached on bank shots. Splendid Splinter was a lot of fun to work with; his constant jokes and humor helped Preston get through the six-week training period. Splinter was skinny as a rail, and he had more wrinkles on his seventy-nine-year-old face than a Shar Pei.

The six weeks passed quickly, and Preston would now be able to enjoy a week off. His last training session ended at noon. After a wonderful lunch, Preston headed for the MGM Grand for a little fun at the poker tables. One of Preston's favorite pastimes was pot-limit poker. Whenever he had a chance, which wasn't often, he would join in a game. After just two hours of playing, he found himself nearly six thousand down.

There was one thing he hated about playing poker in the states; too much jabbering was allowed. There was constant talk. If you spoke too much in England you would forfeit the hand, but this wasn't the American way. On this particular afternoon a lean cowboy in his late sixties wouldn't shut up. He wore a bright red Weston suit, with a bolo around his neck displaying a royal straight flush. On his head sat a big Western hat with a rattlesnake skin wrapped around the brim. He kept talked more than anybody Preston had ever played, and he irritated Preston even more by winning.

The constant yapping kept on, and it seemed to be aimed at Preston. "Yes siree, I do declare," the man stated, chain smoking Winston cigarettes, "This fine English gentleman over here baited me and won. I'll guarantee you that not all trappers wear fur coats"

Preston, still losing, was getting a little restless. Texas hold 'em was a good gambling game as it allowed for a lot of bluffing. Each player was dealt two cards; then three cards were turned up in the middle of the table. After a round of betting another card was flipped, and finally one more card in the last round. The best five cards formed to make a hand. It was basically seven card stud, except all the players played the five cards in the middle.

On the next deal, Preston was dealt the seven and eight of hearts. The betting resulted in a thousand dollar bet from the Texan. Preston called. On the turn the queen of hearts appeared, along with a five of hearts and a nine of spades. With a possible heart flush drawn, Preston called all bets. When it was the Texan's turn, he raised three thousand. Preston called again. The next card up was an ace of clubs. There were only two players left in the hand now: the Texan and Preston. The Texan bet four thousand. Preston guessed he was bluffing, or that he might have two queens.

Preston hadn't bluffed during the whole game; he figured this would be a good time to represent aces. If it failed, he still had a flush draw. Preston called and raised five thousand. "Well, lookie here," the Texan rattled. "We got us a live English gentleman." The Texan grabbed and shoved all his chips forward. "I call you, and I raise what I have left: $7,300." The Texan leaned back, puffing on his cigarette, which had almost burned down to the filter.

"I call $6,400. That's all I have," Preston said. He didn't like the re-raise. He had misjudged his opponent's hand. The bluff had failed. Now all he could do is hope for a heart or a lucky six, to give him a straight. The next card up was a seemingly inconsequential six of spades. The Texan, assuming the six of spades was of no help to the Englishman, smirked. He pitched over his pocket queens and declared, "Three little mop squeezers ought to do the trick." The Texan reached for the chips.

Preston stalled for a second, just to rub it in. "That's a good hand, my friend. But that six of spades gave me an inside straight."

The Texan couldn't believe it. He leaned back in his chair, shaking his head and complaining. "Hell, any ol' six would have done it. It could have been a six of diamonds, or hell, even the six of clubs. Just any ol' six." The Texan continued shaking his head. "Better to be lucky than good."

Behind the dealer, Preston observed a heavyset man walking briskly through the room and out the opposite hallway. "That's Cue himself," he mumbled. "I'll be damned." He was gathering his massive stacks of chips when a man tapped him on the shoulder. "The Colonel wants you to call him as soon as possible." The man handed him a note and walked away.

"Excuse me, gentlemen, but I must call it an afternoon." Preston turned away from the table to read the note:

MEET ME MONDAY MORNING AT 9:40
ON THE FIRST TEE OF THE OLD COURSE AT ST.
ANDREWS.—THE COLONEL

"Damn it," Preston muttered. 9:40 meant 5:40 in the Colonel's code. All stated times were four hours earlier than the intended rendezvous. "Well, there goes my relaxing week in Vegas."

Something important must have come up for the Colonel to interrupt his vacation. "Why so damn early?" Preston headed toward the hall that Dr. Cue had entered. Peeking around the corner, he saw Cue involved in an exhibition match. Preston watched for a while, careful not to be noticed by Cue. He was good, Preston decided, and he constantly broke up the small gallery with his comical cracks and humorous jabs. "Damn, what a time to have to leave," Preston mumbled. "Just when things were starting to get interesting."

CHAPTER SIX

Preston rose early that morning. The weather was not to his liking: cold with a slight mist, and very windy. Some gusts reached thirty miles an hour. If you were going to play golf in Scotland, particularly at the seaside links courses, you learned to accept the wind. It was always present, but this morning it worse than usual. Preston made damn sure he was dressed warmly in a turtleneck, a cashmere sweater, a windbreaker, and a wool stocking cap. Playing in the cold was not one of his favorite things to do, and the wind made it even more dreadful.

"Why the hell are we playing at 5:30 in the morning?" Preston muttered to himself as he walked toward the first tee box. In the background the stone clubhouse, built years ago, towered over him. In Scotland during the summer, daylight lasted from four in the morning to almost eleven at night.

Preston approached the Colonel, waiting with his ball already teed up. He seemed anxious to start; patience was not one of the Colonel's virtues. "Good morning. Preston. Let's get started before someone else shows up."

In charcoal gray knickers with brightly colored argyle socks, the Colonel was a sight to see—a true lover of the game. He wore a navy turtleneck under a heavy red sweater. Beneath a Ben Hogan-style gray tweed hat, his usual cigar was present. He looked like a fashion-conscious guerilla, Preston concluded.

The Colonel took a short backswing and struck the ball with all 230 pounds of his weight. "Another damn slice," the Colonel moaned as his ball almost went out of bounds to the right. "Oh, what the hell. One of these days, I'm going to have to learn to correct it."

They played quickly. The mist continued to hover but never turned into anything more. The wind blew and blew, sometimes gusting to thirty-five miles per hour. Their faces were red as beets. The wind didn't seem to faze the Colonel, but Preston had just as soon the round be over.

Still, there was something magical about this golf course; it was like walking through history. Every hole had its own name. The fourth hole was called "Ginger Beer," and the tenth was the Bobby Jones hole. The most famous of the lot was the treacherous Road Hole, a 461-yard par four that played like a par five. Many championships had been lost as the result of this hole; Preston remembered a fellow by the name of Taylor taking a thirteen on the hole years ago, which cost him the victory.

Many of the bunkers also had names: Hell bunker, the Coffin bunkers, the Stoke bunker. The dreaded Hill bunker, located on the eleventh hole, was nearly ten feet deep. A man could disappear in that one if he weren't careful.

After a while, Preston loosened up and began to enjoy the round more. The course was so historical that it finally took Preston's mind away from the cold and the wind. Neither of them bothered to keep score, and only an occasional par was made. Birdies were not to be found. At the eleventh, a 112-yard par 3, both men managed to hit their drives into the dreaded Hill bunker. The wind blew directly into their faces, so severely that both men were forced to hit drivers from the middle of the teeing area.

After they had managed to blast their way out of the monstrous bunker, the Colonel beckoned Preston with his arm. "Come over here for a minute. Let's take a break. Leave the bags."

Such a cautious man, Preston mused. No golf bags nearby—probably in fear that they might be bugged. Here they were at six-thirty in the morning, at the farthest point from the clubhouse, with absolutely no human beings in sight, with nothing around but the eeriness of the golf course. No trees anywhere, nothing but sand, bunkers, and grisly little yellow bushes. Behind the green was the bank of the River Eden, which flowed into St. Andrew's Bay. The only noises were the wind howling through the bushes and the waves slapping the bank of the river behind them. They knelt beside the bunker as the Colonel talked.

"Preston, something interesting has come up that has changed our plans a little bit. Bela and Cue's father committed suicide Saturday morning. The funeral will be held in Switzerland on Wednesday. Somehow the Swiss are allowing Bela to leave the jail to attend the funeral. Of course, he will be heavily guarded, but nevertheless a stupid decision on somebody's part. I imagine our friend Cue had something to do with this—probably a payoff or something.

"Anyhow, we have reason to suspect there could be an escape plan in the works, but we don't know for sure. For one thing, we have reason to believe Bela had his father killed and made it look like a suicide." The Colonel shook his head. "A nice little chap isn't he? Killing his own father so he can plan an escape. Our sources tell me he will be flown by helicopter to a small cemetery located high on a hill in the middle of nowhere, not far from Interlaken, Switzerland. There the funeral will take place."

The Colonel stood up, stretched a bit, and relit his cigar, covering his lighter with his sweater so it wouldn't keep blowing out. "Preston, I want you to fly up there tomorrow and find a good observation point before the funeral starts. Do not interfere if there's an escape, but try to follow them if you can. I've already arranged for your travel. I have a hunch we're going to uncover something sooner or later about these two that will shock the hell out of us." The Colonel walked toward his golf bag. "Let's finish the round."

"Was that all there was to it?" Preston asked himself. "I flew all the way to St. Andrews to hear this simple request? My, but the Colonel is a tough one to figure."

The back nine played downwind, which made the holes much easier. Preston had even managed to birdie sixteen and eighteen, which were short par fours—particularly with a twenty- to thirty-mile-an-hour wind in their favor. On the seventeenth hole, a boy on a motor scooter drove up and to collect their green fees. Such were the ways of Scotland.

CHAPTER SEVEN

"What a serene setting to be buried in," Preston mused. "Out here in the middle of nowhere." It was Wednesday afternoon, a half hour from when the funeral was scheduled to begin in the quaint country cemetery, nestled near a valley of tall grass, pines, and beautiful wildflowers. The Swiss Alps towered above. The air smelled clean and fresh in the peaceful countryside. All was still but for the rushing sound of water from a nearby brook, gurgling its way beside a narrow rocky mountain path to the lake below.

Preston had parked his rental car down the hill in a small grove of pines, being cautious not to arouse suspicion in the desolate countryside. After walking a mile uphill to the cemetery, Preston spent several minutes shimmying his way up the side of a mausoleum not far from the burial site. The climb took longer than it normally would have, because of Preston's attire: gray slacks, a sweater, and a sport coat. This was not exactly his preferred climbing outfit, but it was a wise precaution. He believed it was better to be overdressed than underdressed; he never knew what situation would arise.

Preston laid on his stomach for an hour, stretched on top of the mausoleum. Peering through the carvings, he used his binoculars to observe the cemetery and the freshly dug grave. He scanned the countryside, but his search produced no trace of activity. Not a single car passed along the valley road.

"Where the hell are you?" he complained. "You're late." He grew tired from the boredom. It was all he could do to stay awake. He, knelt on his knees, moved his arms back and forth, and slapped his face lightly. "A cup of coffee, please," Preston muttered. Another fifteen minutes passed; still there was no sign of anyone. He grew restless.

"Come on, dammit, where the hell are you?" Uncomfortable thoughts began to race through his mind. He started to doubt that the funeral would even take place. Perhaps it had been cancelled or postponed until tomorrow. "Christ, please not that. I can't bear the thought of lying up here all day with no clue if this damn thing will ever take place."

Ignoring his instincts, he removed a cigarette from his case. "Never take unnecessary chances, no matter how safe you think you are," he reminded himself. He stared at the cigarette for a moment, twisting it between his fingers, waiting to see if temptation would win over good judgement. "Oh, what the hell," he mumbled. But before he could light the cigarette, he noticed movement far down the valley road.

Using his binoculars, Preston observed a two-car funeral procession: a black hearse followed by a black Mercedes. He watched the short procession make its journey along the winding valley road until it arrived at the grave. By now, the Mercedes was close enough that Preston could recognize the driver. It was Cue.

But where was Cue's brother? Preston now heard the loud whipping sound of a helicopter, approaching from behind. For a moment he had the sudden sensation the chopper would execute a rooftop landing on the mausoleum. "Dammit," he moaned, crouching between the carvings. The chopper passed overhead; Preston felt the wind whistle around him.

He waited until the police helicopter landed before he rose to get a better look. Three uniformed policemen and a man in a dark suit, his hands cuffed from behind him, crawled out from beneath the blades. "That's our nice chap," Preston mused. "We've been wondering where you were." He studied Bela with his binoculars; he was a short, thin man with a pencil mustache, deep-set brown eyes, coal-black hair cropped close, and a face that probably hadn't produced a smile in years.

A Catholic priest and one more uniformed policeman got out of the hearse—no burial detail anywhere. Preston guessed the policemen would be the pallbearers. Cue's Mercedes was parked not far behind the hearse, but the occupants remained in the car.

"How odd," Preston noted. "Why won't they get out?" His eyes switched to the four pallbearers, all policemen armed with small machine guns, as they carried the casket up the incline and placed it next to the open grave.

"Interesting," Preston muttered. "The pallbearers never met the man they're about to bury." Preston's wondered how this escape was going to take place. He scanned the countryside for activity, but there was none. Where were Bela's accomplices? How the hell was he going to pull this off?

He eyed the Mercedes with his binoculars. At last the doors opened. Cue was the first one out, followed by an elderly woman whom Preston guessed was his mother. A woman exited the vehicle and walked slowly behind Cue and his mother. Preston couldn't see the women's face—a black scarf covered up most of it. "It has to be a sister," he decided.

The three approached the graveside, standing opposite the four policemen who were guarding Bela from each side.

A heavyset, white-haired priest approached and began his eulogy. Preston couldn't get over how odd the funeral was: four armed policemen and Bela, a suspected murderer and convicted drug dealer, along with a smooth-talking pool hustler, a lonely mother, and an unknown woman.

There was something about this other woman. He'd been watching Bela to see what he might be up to, but Preston kept shifting the binoculars to her. Finally his curiosity was answered when she turned her head toward the mausoleum. "It can't be!" Preston blurted she removed her black scarf. "You must be kidding . . ." A smile crossed his lips. "If it isn't my darling runaway, Sabrina. What on earth is she doing here?" A friend of Bela's? A relative? Surely she's not Cue's girl"—Preston refused to accept that possibility—"too much class for him."

Preston could hardly accept that Sabrina was now in his sight; his eyes sparkled with pleasure. He listened as the priest began the graveside service, but he was too far away to hear what he was saying. Now was the time for Preston to take the proceedings more seriously; the escape would have to take place in the next few minutes.

Preston put his binoculars on the guards. He doubted any of them would be involved in Bela's escape. But who knew who could be involved? The priest? His mother? Cue? Sabrina? It didn't make sense that four heavily armed policemen were the only ones attending the funeral besides the priest, Cue and his mother and brother, and Sabrina.

No one else was in sight anywhere. He couldn't figure it out—maybe the escape was canceled. But the Colonel rarely miscalculated. Preston thought maybe Bela's escape would occur on the helicopter ride back to the prison.

The priest, open Bible in hand, continued his readings. Preston guessed the funeral would end shortly. He focused on Bela but still couldn't get a good look at him. "Dammit," Preston groaned, wishing he could see his facial expression. He turned his attention to Cue, looking for a sign. Cue offered none. He shifted the binoculars to Sabrina and studied her face. She showed no emotion, no grief or sorrow; if anything, she appeared bored with the afternoon's events.

Preston moved his feet back and forth in a nervous gesture. Suddenly, without warning, Bela lunged forward, his hands still cuffed, and fell into the open grave. The guards, stunned, managed to regain their composure and simultaneously pointed their weapons toward the empty grave.

On the other side of the hole, two small squares about the size of a car's hubcaps popped open on the side of the casket. Before the guards could react, two machine gun barrels protruded from the open square holes. The mountain air crackled with machine gun fire; smoke and sparks flew in every direction.

The guards never had a chance. The gruesome, close-range massacre happened quickly and precisely.

Round after round whistled from the two machine guns, shredding the flesh of their helpless targets. The four dead policemen were little more than human sieves now. Their final screams of agony echoed through the valley and off the distant mountains. These faded echoes were soon replaced by an eerie silence. No one moved; those who had survived the killings froze in shock. Preston lay dazed, dumbfounded by what he had witnessed. It happened so fast that it didn't seem real.

Preston figured they would probably murder the priest next to keep him from talking. The thought repulsed Preston. He felt helpless. He wanted to do something so badly, but he knew there was nothing he could do; he had no chance to intervene.

"Damn it, give me a high powered rifle. Then I'll show them a thing or two." Preston's attention turned to the top of the casket, which lifted open from the inside. Two short men in black tights and ski masks crawled out, carrying small machine guns.

"The honored funeral guest isn't even here." Preston couldn't believe it. "I'll be damned." The two men reached down and pulled Bela out of the open grave. They removed the handcuff keys from one of the dead guards and freed his hands.

"Let's get the hell out of here," Bela ordered. The priest pitched his Bible into the grave, and ripped off his white collar. The four of them rushed over to the black hearse, loading up. Bela drove the hearse down the narrow road.

Preston turned his attention to Cue who, with his mother and Sabrina, calmly walked to his Mercedes. They soon departed down the same road, considerably far back from the hearse, driving so slow that it appeared that they were going for a Sunday drive.

"Such a cool cucumber, that Cue," Preston noted. "A real slick little devil. And what about Sabrina? She's obviously a close relative or sister—or Cue's girl." Preston did not want to believe that last option. His immediate priority was to find some way of tracking them before they got too far away. But by the time he hiked back to his car, it would be too late.

There was only one alternative: the police helicopter.

Preston hadn't operated a helicopter since his British Secret Service days, and he wondered if he could remember enough about the bloody machine to keep it up in the air. He climbed down from the mausoleum and sprinted to the helicopter.

"Damn cigarettes," Preston complained, short of breath. After a few nervous minutes, most of his training returned to him. Soon he was high above the ground, and after a few minutes of flying along the winding mountain road, using his binoculars, he was able to spot Cue's Mercedes in the far distance. But the hearse was long gone. Staying high above and far back so he wouldn't be detected, Preston followed Cue for almost two hours, watching the Mercedes twist and turn through the mountain valley. His fuel gauge was getting precariously low-he guessed he had about thirty minutes of flight time left. Preston muttered, "Just where the hell is Cue going?"

Finally Cue turned off the narrow mountain road and drove toward a large mountain resort. Preston lost sight of the Mercedes as Cue drove through the iron gates of the grand old hotel. He wondered where he could land; he needed someplace flat and safe, far enough from the hotel to not cause a scene. Flying over the beautiful twelve-story stone building, he noticed a small heliport to the east of the hotel.

It was nearly dark and Preston, who did not have instrument training, didn't want to fly the chopper at night. He knew he couldn't stay up much longer, but there was too much activity at the heliport for him to land. So he decided to kill a few minutes by flying near the snowcapped mountain not far from the hotel. Soon, nightfall descended and his fuel gauge showed almost empty. He had no choice but to land on his next swing back around.

Preston was relieved to see that the activity on the heliport had quieted. It was almost pitch dark now. Preston, in a hurry to land, came down fast—the mountain crosswind was stronger than he had anticipated. He slammed the helicopter hard onto the heliport, bending the landing gear. An attendant rushed over to the helicopter.

"Sir, are you all right?"

"No problem," Preston assured him. "I never was much good at hovering." Departing hastily, he approached a small outdoor dining area leading up to two tall, hand-carved wooden doors. He pulled them open and entered the hotel.

Before him he saw an impressive game room. The chandeliers above were made from antlers. Across the room, a large stone fireplace burned with bright red flames. "Those logs must be five feet long," Preston observed. The fire warmed the five card players seated not far from it. Beautiful mahogany card tables and hand-carved chairs were scattered through the large room.

On the east side he glimpsed several snooker and pool tables. On the south end of the game room there was a magnificent bar that must have been broken down and transported overseas from an old Western saloon in the US Elaborately carved, it was as fancy a bar as Preston had ever seen. "Wyatt Earp would have approved," Preston guessed.

The game room was unusually quiet, and Preston wondered why it was so empty. "Mr. Hardin, I presume?" A stocky older man stood up and waved him over to their table.

"I'll be damned," Preston muttered. "If it isn't Dr. Cue himself."

"Come and join us. So glad you accepted my invitation."

"Why, yes I am Mr. Hardin," Preston answered. "Much obliged for your kind invitation. I look forward to the evening's entertainment. Sorry I'm late; my plane was delayed." Preston approached the table, shook hands with Cue, and sat down in the empty chair across from the man. After all introductions around the table were over, Preston was handed twenty thousand in chips. He scribbled on a sheet the bartender handed him.

Cue spoke: "As you have been earlier informed, the only game we play tonight is five-card stud. I've been told you are one of the best."

"Well," Preston answered, "things can get exaggerated." He took a deep drag from his cigarette and watched as the cards were dealt around the table. By the time the fourth round of cards were dealt, there were only two players left in the game: Cue and himself. Cue's down card was a two of spades. He showed the four, five, and six of diamonds. Preston's down card was the queen of spades, and his three showing cards were the king of clubs, two of hearts, and the jack of hearts.

"Four thousand is my bet," said Cue.

Preston reluctantly called. Still, he knew that he had three face cards that could be paired up. The final cards were dealt: the eight of diamonds was dealt to Cue, the five of clubs came to Preston. Cue smiled and bet seven thousand, certain there was no way Preston would call with a possible flush and inside straight draw staring at him.

Preston lit another cigarette, studied Cue's hand movements, and watched his eyes for any sign of nervousness. He was in no hurry. "Well," Cue finally blurted, "are we in or are we out?"

Preston gave a small grin. "I call."

Cue, shocked, hesitated a bit, knowing there was no way he could win. "What do you have?" Cue asked.

Preston, having determined that he'd lost the hand, casually answered: "Kings."

"How many?" Cue asked, irritated.

"One." Preston thought he would play a little game with Cue.

"That's good," Cue grabbed his cards. In a fit of rage, he threw his cards across the table. "Nobody but a fool would call a seven-thousand dollar bet with a worthless hand like yours—and with a hand like mine staring down his throat."

"Your eyes gave you away, Dr. Cue. Plus, you bet too much," Preston said. "If you had made a smaller bet, I wouldn't have called." Preston threw that in just to irritate Cue. Before anything more could be said, a man entered the room. Preston knew his stay was going to end soon.

"Good evening, gentlemen. I am Guy Hardin. It doesn't appear you've saved me a seat. I apologize for my tardiness, but I was detained at the airport."

Preston rose quickly. "Allow me to offer you my chair. I seemed to have overplayed my hand tonight." He turned to Cue: "Please mail my winnings to my mother, if you don't mind. I must be going." He backtracked toward the north exit.

Cue turned to the heavyset bartender. "Stop him, now."

Before Preston could exit, the bartender lunged at him and struck his hand across the back of Preston's neck. Preston fell to his knees, reached inside his coat, pulled out his Beretta and pointed it at the bartender's face. The bartender retreated. Preston rushed to the large door and ran out into the hallway. Behind him he could hear Dr. Cue shouting, "Kill him!"

Preston ran down the hall and turned the corner. Two men came toward him. He started down the other wing and ran up two flights of stairs before entering another hallway. The footsteps of several men pounded on the stairs in pursuit. Preston attempted to open several guest room doors as he ran down the hallway; he finally found one that wasn't locked.

Preston locked the door behind him and raced to the balcony. Outside, he didn't like what he saw. It was a straight drop, several stories down—there was no way he could survive the jump. The other balconies were too far away. The men outside kicked hard at the door.

Preston knew even those heavy doors wouldn't hold much longer. He figured the best he could do was to either shoot it out or surrender. The latter didn't seem too appealing, considering what Cue had shouted earlier: "Kill him!"

Preston cursed himself for being so careless. "Never allow yourself to be trapped," he repeated to himself. He should never have entered the room. Instead, he should have continued down the hall until he saw an outside exit. The pounding on the door grew louder. The door splintered.

Preston reached for his Beretta. There was no other choice but to shoot and hope for the best. Suddenly, Preston heard a woman's voice call to him from the balcony above: "Grab the rope and climb up."

He couldn't believe what he was seeing. It was Sabrina. What the hell was she doing with a climbing rope?

"Grab the rope, Preston. Hurry . . ." Sabrina urged, "before it's too late."

Preston grabbed the rope. With the aid of Sabrina, he climbed as fast as possible, crawling over the stone ledge. Preston heard his pursuers enter the balcony below. He and Sabrina lay flat on the floor, careful not to make any noise. Preston hoped his pursuers would guess he had jumped.

Sabrina coiled the rope. They entered the hotel room, closing the doors behind them. Turning to Preston, she asked for a cigarette. After Preston had lit her up, she sat down on the four-poster bed. With a flirtatious gleam in her eyes, she said: "Now we're even, Mr. James."

"Yes, we area at that." Preston lit a cigarette and studied the white silk nightgown Sabrina wore. "What the devil are you doing with mountain gear in your room? Are they replacing Gideon bibles with climbing ropes now?"

"It's my hobby, Mr. James. I climb extensively," Sabrina said. "I plan to climb tomorrow, not far from here."

"What other hobbies do you have, Sabrina?" He undressed her with his eyes.

"Cool your jets," she said. "You're wasting your energies."

"What about Cue. Does he waste his energies?" Preston asked.

"That's none of your business, Mr. James." Sabrina puffed on her cigarette. Her eyes squinted at Preston. "You seem to have a problem dealing with your rude manners."

"You're correct," Preston answered. "I apologize. I have a few questions I would like to ask you . . ."

"Some other time. Sebastian could be here any minute. You must leave now. You can cross the hall; there's an exit close by that will take you down the fire escape."

"When can I see you again?" Preston asked.

Dr. Cue

"Meet me tomorrow at two o'clock, at the top of the small mountain behind the white chapel east of town. It's about five miles away. There's only one road out of town; you can't get lost. After you pass the chapel, follow the road until it dead ends. Then you'll take a lengthy hike, following the only trail that leads to the top. I'm going to climb up from the west side with my gear—it's very steep, almost straight up. Here's the key to my red BMW. When you get to the valet parking, ask for Roger. He's my friend, and he'll help you. He also keeps his mouth shut. Be careful leaving town. I can't afford to have Sebastian's henchmen seeing you in my car. You must go. Good night and be careful. Roger will give me a ride tomorrow. Also bring some lunch, and red wine and mineral water."

Preston managed a quiet escape. As instructed, he drove off in Sabrina's red BMW. After driving to a nearby village, he was determined to spend the final hours of the night in total relaxation. He checked into a cozy pension and showered, starting with very hot water at first, and finishing with the coldest spray of water his body could tolerate.

Later, he enjoyed a grilled fish dinner at a nearby cafe, complimenting his meal with the finest white wine the café offered. Preston then returned to his room, and within minutes he fell into a deep sleep that continued without interruption through the night until the bright, narrow rays of the morning sun shined through the window next to his bed.

Preston checked his watch: 9:35. This was a rare treat. Preston seldom got eight hours in one night, and he

70

rarely slept past seven. Preston spent the rest of the morning outfitting himself at a local clothing shop. He rounded up two bottles of red wine, cheese, bread, and ham for his awaited luncheon with Sabrina. Returning to his pension, he showered and dressed, then set out for his afternoon rendezvous with Sabrina.

With the village behind him, Preston drove down the narrow valley road and turned the BMW to his right as he'd been instructed. He passed the country church with its high wooden steeple, and began his slow ascent up the mountain.

A rushing river, formed from the melting snow, carved a winding path down the valley floor. On the other side of the river, some distance away, were rows of mountains. Smaller ones in the foreground gave way to towering mountains in the back. Occasional water spouts gushed from the mountain above, making their narrow journey down to the river below. Mist rose high as the mountain water splashed onto the rocks below. This time of the year, everything appeared so green. The landscape was so vivid with color, so richly displayed, particularly when the sun hid behind the clouds. It was the perfect backdrop for the mountain flowers that flaunted their vibrant colors. Small houses and herds of dairy cows were scattered among the mountain valley.

"Little farms in the sky," Preston mused, "This is definitely God's country."

He continued up the curvaceous, two-lane mountain road, occasionally pulling over to allow tourist buses to pass by. Preston turned the radio on. Mozart's "A Light Night Music" was playing. Preston negotiated a hairpin curve, dropped into a lower gear, and continued up the road.

"Not much longer . . . But what about Sabrina?" he asked himself. Why did she intrigue him so? There were so many questions left to be answered. He had to be on full alert; this woman was extraordinary, quick-minded and intelligent. Preston was not going to allow her to get the best of him. He'd had three short encounters with the lady, in such unusual circumstances—so coincidental. Preston's mind flashed back to last summer. The similarities were there with his affair with Tanya: too many coincidental happenings, too many chance meetings.

He pushed the similarities from his mind. He didn't want to believe this could happen with Sabrina. Never before had a woman so aroused his curiosity by her manner and conduct. God knew he'd dealt with enough women in his twenty years of service—every possible kind, from sluts to spies, from paupers to princesses, dizzy blondes and calculating killers, sex goddesses and lesbians, saints and bitches.

"My God," Preston blurted. "I still have nightmares about some of these women. I've seen them all, the sweet, the cute, the beautiful, the sensuous, the elegant, the greedy, the ruthless and . . . the most disgusting of them all: the coldblooded killer, who enjoys murdering her prey."

"What is this one going to be?" Preston asked himself. "I can't keep getting dealt bad hands." But then again, sometimes luck ran in streaks. After all, she did save his life back at the hotel, and probably risked hers in doing so. He lit a cigarette and reminded himself to keep up his guard.

"Trust no one," was a phrase Preston constantly repeated to himself. His thoughts returned to Sabrina. Why was she so upset at his first encounter with her, at the outdoor café on the Champs Elysees? It had been more than a simple brushoff; instinct had taught Preston that. Was it because she feared Cue? Then who the hell was trying to kill her, and why? Cue didn't have time to pull this off. So, why did she suddenly disappear? How heavily involved was she with Cue? Was she his lover, or just a companion? Had she been aware of Bela's escape plan? Cue was very clever to arrive late and to distance himself from the slaughter and the escape.

"Maybe she does love him." Preston didn't want to accept that thought. "But if that were true, why would Sabrina help him escape?"

"No more mistakes, Preston." He could hear those words coming from the Colonel, as if the man were sitting in the car next to him. After this summer's fiasco, the Colonel's patience was growing thin. "Damn," he mumbled. At first he couldn't wait for his romantic rendezvous. But now he'd psyched himself up to the point where he did not know whether to romance this woman or wish her gone.

Reaching the dead end, he turned off the road and parked the car in a small grove of trees. Preston loaded the backpack, hooked it onto his back, and began climbing the lone path ahead. Thirty minutes later, having zigzagged his way up the rocky path, he finally reached the top, which was about half the size of a soccer field. The panorama was breathtaking.

Preston approached two dwarf cedars. Unfolding a neatly packed blanket, he spread out the snacks, and opened both bottles of wine to allow them to breathe. Then he walked over to the west end of the mountaintop to await Sabrina's arrival. Below, the mountain's west face rose almost in a vertical angle. It was composed mostly of jagged stone and was much steeper than its surrounding environment. It was a healthy climb for most mountain climbers, but would be little challenge to a seasoned climber, such as the one who was now finishing her final ascent.

"Good afternoon," Preston said as Sabrina pulled herself up past the final ledge. She squatted, resting her arms on her knees, and wiped the perspiration from her face with a handkerchief. Sabrina wore a simple outfit: pleated khaki shorts, a bright pink shirt, green suspenders, heavy striped socks that ended just below her knees, and Vasque climbing boots.

"You're fifteen minutes late. Where have you been?" Preston asked. Sabrina, looking at Preston with humorous contempt, offered no reply. Flashing a slight smile, she walked toward the picnic blanket. Without turning her head or slowing her pace, she said: "Is my lunch ready? Surely you thought to bring mineral water?"

Preston, walking behind her, replied: "Yes, dear. Everything is prepared and awaiting your approval."

Sabrina removed her climbing gear, knelt down, picked up a water bottle and guzzled it. With a sigh of relief, she wiped her forehead and turned her attention to Preston. "Are you a good housekeeper too?"

Preston had expected this playful needling from her. After all, this was a classic role reversal that had begun when she rescued him at the hotel. He played along: "I can cook and wash with the best of them."

He sat down next to her, picked up the bottle of wine, and poured two glasses. Offering one to her, he raised his glass started a toast: "Here's to a beautiful woman in a very beautiful—" before he finished, he interrupted himself: "I seem to recall those words from somewhere."

He stared hard into Sabrina's eyes. "It's going to be more difficult for you to escape this time, you know . . ." He grinned, his eyes sparkling. Without allowing Sabrina time for a comeback, he said: "Let's have lunch."

Sabrina wasted little time in consuming healthy portions of the ham sandwiches, quenching her thirst with mineral water and red wine. A few minutes later, having finishing their lunch, they rested against the cedar trees. Preston lit two cigarettes and placed one in her mouth. "We need to quit these nasty things one of these days," he warned.

"I ration myself to only six a day," she replied. "Strictly enforced."

"Tell me about yourself. Everything. From the beginning." Preston turned sideways to observe her more closely.

Crossing her legs, Sabrina put her thumbs behind her suspenders, flipping them forward over and over again. "I was raised in the states. Grew up in Washington D.C. My father was a correspondent for NBC. We moved around quite a bit when I was young: London, Paris, New York. I attended the University of Virginia, graduating with a master's degree in psychology. I was a Phi Beta Kappa.

"I was also a prima ballerina and would have made it a career, had I not fallen in love. After graduating, I lived with a man for five years. Sean was his name. I was madly in love with him, but he wouldn't marry me. It ended in Las Vegas."

She stalled for a moment, placing her arms around her knees. "I was jilted, so to speak. Another girl. It was a devastating blow. For so long, everything had come easy to me: school, athletics, ballet, popularity, you name it. I even excelled at mountain climbing. I was so accustomed to having anything I desired. He was the only thing I couldn't have." Sadness fell across her face. She reached for another cigarette, lighting it before Preston could pull out his lighter.

Taking another sip of wine, she continued: "Anyhow, I lived in Las Vegas for quite a while, earning a living as a dancer. I don't know why I stayed—probably because I still felt his presence there, even though he'd left for good. Besides, I enjoyed the excitement of the Las Vegas nightlife.

"I was the only daughter of three children. Through my tomboy years as a teenager, I learned to play a pretty mean game of pool. I excelled in the game, just as I did in mountain climbing. I always loved a challenge. Anyway, I continued on with very little meaning in my life. My first real failure, losing Sean, was too much of a shock to cope with. I continued dancing, and took up pool again. I entered a few tournaments just for the hell of it, and I did very well. This lovesick existence continued for nearly a year, until I met Sebastian during a mixed pool tournament." Preston listened carefully but skeptically.

Sabrina continued: "From that point on, my life took an abrupt change. Even though he was so much older, it was refreshing to be with this man. He was talented, brilliant, entertaining. He had a wonderful sense of humor. He made me feel important. After a year of misery, my life became meaningful again. That was eight months ago. I moved to Switzerland to live with him."

She paused, deep in thought. Her eyes brightened. "He's been so kind to me. He takes me all over the world with him. He surprises me with expensive jewelry and fine clothes. However . . ." Her voice grew more serious. "When we're at the castle, he becomes reclusive. Except for the evenings when we shoot pool, he seems very distant." Sabrina paused, stretching her arms out.

Preston asked: "Do you love him?" He watched her carefully, looking for the signs of deceit he'd been trained to recognize. Some of these signs were simple: the hand covering the mouth, for example, or a quick touch below the nose, along with twitching, increased blinking, excessive perspiration, change in one's pupils, or turning the palms inward. There were also major giveaways, like rubbing one's eyes, or looking away. Preston had mastered this skill, but Sabrina wasn't going to be an easy subject. After all, she was trained in psychology.

But Sabrina didn't answer his question.

"Do you love him?" he repeated.

Her silence continued. She finally said: "I don't know." She shook her head. "I don't know if I'm capable of loving anybody anymore. I gave it all before—only to lose it all. That lovesick feeling, I'll never forget it. It was like someone ripped my stomach out of my body. I don't know that I could handle that feeling again."

Preston watched every hand movement, every facial gesture. "Does he love you?"

"He's very eccentric. A genius, with an incredible personality."

"And . . . does he love you?"

"Please, allow me to finish," she said. "He's always the life of the party. He constantly amuses and entertains those around him. Everybody loves him: the hat check girls, the airline security personnel, the stewardesses—everybody. I've never seen him frown or show displeasure in public. And he never ceases to amaze me with his talents" She gazed upward in thought. "However, behind this super-personality that never seems to falter, there's another person, another personality, as if he were merely an expert actor. Away from the public eye he's much quieter, less tolerant, and sometimes hostile— but never toward me. He treats me with kindness. But sometimes when we shoot pool together, I feel like . . . like I'm playing with a total stranger."

"Do you make love to him?" Preston asked reluctantly, fearing the worst.

"Why bother to say anything." She spoke in a low tone. "You won't believe me."

"Try me."

"He's never made any romantic gestures toward me, other than small shows of affection in public. We sleep in different bedrooms at the castle, and in separate beds when we're traveling. Sometimes I feel that he's just using me to show me off in public." She turned and faced him. "Which is fine with me. I wouldn't make love to him, even if he wanted me to, but at times it makes me question my own sexuality. This has been going on for over eight months. I'm starting to feel like less of a woman." She giggled. "Imagine me, being insecure about that. How quickly the tables turn."

Preston smiled. Sabrina went on: "For eight months I have lived with a man who does not desire my body, who does not want to make love too me. However, sometimes when we're at the castle I'll catch him watching me swim nude. Just . . . staring. He shows no emotion, and has said nothing to me about it. It's eerie, it makes me feel uncomfortable. I am not prudish about my body; I have a European viewpoint— nudity is natural and beautiful. But this is different. I don't know what the mind behind that cold stare is thinking. So I quit swimming nude and started wearing swimsuits."

Sabrina let another cigarette, showing a puzzled look. "Then, one night after dinner, he made one simple request: 'I want to see you swim as you did before, Sabrina.' That's all he said. He kissed my hand, and after that I didn't see him for the rest of the evening.

"Did you honor his request?" Preston raised his eyebrows in curiosity.

"I saw no reason not to—he's asked so little of me. I think he's earned the right. But it sure gives me the creeps. Sometimes I wonder if he fantasizes that I'm another woman, one that he can't have, someone he lost in the past." Sabrina took another long drag from her cigarette. She poured another glass of wine, took a sip, and continued: "I almost get the impression that he imagines I'm a piece of art or a statue or something. He worships his art so—all of his oil paintings and statues and sculptures are of women. I've always thought that to be a little peculiar."

Sabrina hesitated. "One night . . . without Sebastian knowing of my presence, I watched him dine alone. That wasn't unusual, but this time he was carrying on imaginary conversations with nonexistent guests at the table. I couldn't hear what he was saying, but I saw him gesturing to the empty chairs. This went on for nearly twenty minutes. Finally, he rose from the table and approached a Greek statue. I watched him caress this naked, marble woman, touching her shoulders and face as he talked to her. Again I couldn't make out what he was saying. It frightened me.

"Then, he approached an oil painting that consisted of two maidens bathing nude. Someone famous painted it; I can't remember the name. He talked to the women in the painting, as if they were alive."

"Why do you stay with him?"

"I don't know. He's been so kind to me. He's done so much for me. I'll let it continue for a while, anyway." Sabrina stood up and began stretching her legs, first the left and then the right, back and forth. "I see no reason to end this relationship yet. Except for his occasional strange behavior, I'm having the time of my life. As far as I am concerned, a knight has entered my life and slain the dragon. He may be an eccentric, older knight, but just the same. So, Preston," Sabrina walked about, stretching her arms high in the air. "It's your turn to tell me about you."

"Not yet," he replied. "There are a few more questions I would like to get straight in my mind. First . . . why were you so upset when I sat down at the outdoor café in Paris? That was more than just a simple brush off."

"Sebastian is very jealous," Sabrina explained, "I couldn't afford to be seen with you." Sabrina sat down against the cedar tree. "You're an attractive man, you know?"

Preston showed no reaction. "If Sebastian is so jealous, why did you help me escape? Why would you take a chance on seeing me today?"

"Because I owe you for saving my life. At first, I didn't know how to react, I was so frightened. I could not afford to be caught with you in that mess with the police there. Sebastian would assume we were having an affair." She glanced at him, waiting for a look of satisfaction, but his face remained calm.

"Who tried to kill you?"

"I have no idea. I have no enemies that I'm aware-- none who would go to such lengths. Except perhaps for Bela,

Sebastian's brother." She frowned. "He's evil. Barrymore, Sebastian's butler, tells me more than I should know. He says Bela smuggles drugs. His operation is worldwide. He also told me Bela despises Western culture, and he wouldn't put it past him to be involved in espionage.

Not only is Bela Sebastian's brother, he's also his right hand man. Sebastian considers him a genius. He spends time at the castle, off and on. I've met him several times, but in all of these encounters, he was cool, very aloof—and always suspicious of my relationship with Sebastian. I guess he figures I'm a gold digger, though he ought to know I can pretty much have anybody I want, rich or poor. Or maybe he suspects I'm some type of a spy."

"Final question. The funeral yesterday. Were you aware that the escape had been planned, and that Cue was involved?"

"Where did you hear about that?"

"I was there." Preston replied.

"You couldn't have been. Someone would have seen you."

"I observed the lovely massacre from atop a nearby mausoleum. I'd been nesting there all morning, waiting. Rest assured, my dear, Dr. Cue was fully aware of the escape plan—no doubt Bela and Cue were the masterminds behind it."

"I don't believe it," Sabrina said. "I swear, I knew nothing. I still find it hard to believe Sebastian was involved. He displayed such disgust and shock over the massacre. Perhaps it was an act, but if so, why would he bother to take me there at all?"

"A damn good question. I have no explanation for that one. Perhaps he wanted you there to give you a sense of involvement—a feeling that there's an escape for Bela, but not for Sabrina. I don't know."

"No more questions. Now it's your turn." Sabrina turned and looked at him. "What do you want with Sebastian?"

Preston felt as if she were judging him the same way he had judged her. She was nobody's fool that was for sure. All she had told him was true, or at least that was what he'd concluded through his observations. Not one damn hint of lying. Either she was telling the truth or she was the best liar he'd seen. However, there was something that didn't fit. But he couldn't put his finger on it.

"What do you want with Sebastian?" she asked again.

"I'm a member of an international organization involved in solving art thefts. We have reason to believe Bela and Cue might be involved in a heist. Two irreplaceable Renoir paintings were stolen from a temporary exhibit in

Amsterdam. We strongly suspect their involvement, but we're unable to prove it.

"What are you going to do with them?"

"There's not much we *can* do about them for now; we don't know if they were involved or not. Bela is dangerous. And I think you should seriously consider ending this adventure with Cue. You might find yourself getting involved in situations far beyond your control. You might even be charged as an accomplice. Forget your past, start a new life . . . My God, you have your whole life ahead of you."

"I guess I've always been a sucker for excitement. My life is too entertaining to leave now. I know how to take care of myself."

"If that's your decision, so be it." Preston knew something wasn't right. She was too smart for this; there was no logical reason for her continued involvement with Cue. "I trust that what we've said today will be kept in the strictest of confidence."

"I would have no reason to say anything, even if I wanted to. How could I explain this meeting to Sebastian anyway?"

"One other question. Where does Cue get his money? You don't run around buying lodges, castles, and rare works of art using money from pool winnings."

"He is an international jeweler—an outstanding gem specialist. That's why we make so many trips. It's not just for fun and pool tournaments."

They both sat next to each other silently for a minute, before Preston said: "I don't want to see you get hurt."

"Thanks. As I told you, I can take care of myself."

Preston finished the last drops of wine from his glass and watched the clouds gather, blocking out the sun. Soon it would rain. He took her hand, gently stroking her hair away from her left ear. Then he kissed her lightly on the lips. "Sabrina, you are a beautiful, intelligent woman—"

Sabrina stopped him, releasing the grasp of his hand. She put her arms around his neck and kissed him deeply. Then she leaned back, dropping her arms to her side. She looked at him with no expression, just a mysterious stare from her eyes.

Preston lowered her suspenders from her shoulders, allowing them to fall down her arms. Starting from the top, he unbuttoned her blouse until he reached her waistline, careful not to spread the shirt apart. He stared for a moment at her mysterious eyes. Then, placing his hands inside her blouse, he opened her shirt. Without touching any part of her body, he pulled the shirt halfway down her back, exposing small, well-rounded breasts.

"Make love to me." Sabrina said. Small, cool drops

of water descended from the gray clouds above, falling unnoticed on the two lovers below.

An hour later, the red BMW started its trek down the mountain, but with a different driver than before. Preston lowered his right window and allowed the heavy mist to blow in his face as he watched Sabrina negotiate the curves.

As Sabrina approached the outskirts of the village, she pulled alongside a small barn.

"This is as far as I can take you. I can't risk being seen with you. Hopefully you can pay a villager to give you a ride back to the cemetery."

"Shouldn't be a problem. Everyone has their price."

Sabrina ignored the remark. "Good luck to you. It was a most enjoyable afternoon."

"I don't even know your last name."

"Sabrina Tucker," she answered.

"Funny, it doesn't fit you. It's almost like a dreamed up name for a Hollywood actress."

"Thanks a lot," Sabrina replied.

"Anyway, thanks for saving my life last night. I, too, enjoyed the afternoon's entertainment." Preston smiled. "But now I'm all tuckered out."

"Oh, aren't we a funny little boy? Good day, Preston."

He got out and leaned on the window. "When will I see you again?"

"The next time you get yourself in trouble, give me a call. I might be around to rescue you."

He watched her drive away. Preston walked toward his pension, careful to avoid the main road. He tried to piece together what little he'd learned from his afternoon encounter with Sabrina. He recalled the words of Winston Churchill in reference to the Soviet Union. "She is an enigma wrapped in a riddle wrapped in a cocoon."

"Not one damn lie!" Preston muttered in astonishment. "Not even a deceitful gesture or expression. She was too smooth; generally, by now, his instincts would have revealed enough about her to form some conclusions. But he was even more at a loss after today's encounter than he'd been before. She was too smart to be playing Cue's tagalong trophy girl. "I don't buy that lovesick crap either." He mumbled to himself. On arriving at the pension, he called Winston to report in.

"Where the hell have you been?" the Colonel growled. "Never mind. Meet O'Grady on the front steps of St. Peter's parish church in Zurich. 11:10 sharp, tomorrow night." That meant 7:10.

"Winston would never make it as a telephone solicitor," Preston said after he'd rung off. He looked forward to seeing Mike.

Early the next morning Preston found a ride back to the cemetery. It involved a hefty tip, plus the chore of listening to two hours of nonstop jabbering in broken English from the hired lad, before they finally arrived at their destination.

Hours later, after a tedious mountain drive, Preston arrived at Kloten, Switzerland's largest airport. Dropping off his rental car, he hailed a taxi and headed for his rendezvous with Mike O'Grady at St. Peter's.

Even though it was the economic and cultural hub of Switzerland Zurich wasn't one of his favorite cities. The people that inhabited it weren't his favorite, either. This was a fast moving city, and heavily industrialized. To Preston, it was a giant ant bed of workaholics, money makers, spies, and foreigners. He looked out the taxi's window, watching the people scurrying along, heading for their business deals. These people didn't know the meaning of the word *leisure*. They were always checking their watches or looking up at the large clocks above them. No wonder Swiss timepieces were the best in the world—the Swiss needed them the most. But it wasn't just Zurich; all of Switzerland's major cities were a disappointment—a far cry from the storybook impression Switzerland's tourist bureau so carefully projected to the world. There were no yodelers here, except at the Swiss stock exchange.

Preston lit a cigarette. A frown crossed his face. He slumped in his seat, distressed at the inescapable traffic. No matter how seasoned a driver you were, no matter how many shortcuts you took, the Zurich traffic would be still be waiting for you like the plaque. All incoming motorways ended at the city's outskirts. There were no large thoroughfares through the city; consequently the traffic rumbled through the heart of the city like bumper cars let loose from an amusement park. It was a test of endurance that tried even the most patient souls.

"I would rather cross Lake Zurich lengthwise in a rowboat than drive through this damn town," Preston groaned. He lit another cigarette. Thirty five minutes later, their traffic ordeal finally behind them, the taxi drove alongside the massive Lake Zurich, which extended for miles into the distance.

The sea of freshwater finally brought a smile to Preston's face. Looking across the rich blue waters, he recalled one of his few enjoyable visits to the city—over twenty years ago. 1964 saw Lake Zurich freeze over for the first time since 1920. It was delightful to see; there were thousands of skaters out on the lake, enjoying the rare occurrence. Even Preston, just for the hell of it, had given it a try. It was his first attempt at ice skating, and it would be his last.

His reveries halted as the taxi pulled up to the steps of St. Peter's church. Mike O'Grady approached Preston as he got out of the taxi.

"How the hell are you, Preston? Let's get out of here." Mike O'Grady wasn't your typical agent; in fact he would probably be the last person you would pick as a spy, particularly a former British intelligence officer. He was a red-faced Irishman with a strong Irish accent and red hair. At five-foot-eight he was slightly overweight, but not as heavy as his big-boned structure made him seem. His lumbering walk and floppy arm movements gave the impression of a football coach rather than an intelligence agent. But Winston had become impressed with his past heroics, so Mike had joined the ISS a year ago as their first agent from Ireland.

"Well, Preston, we're on our merry way to the Baur Au Lac hotel, overlooking Lake Zurich."

"Fancy," Preston answered. "But why didn't we meet there? Why the steps at St. Peter's?"

Mike laughed. "You know how Winston is. He didn't want anybody seeing the two of us together. At St. Peter's church, we would have noticed a car tailing us. When we get to the hotel, I'll check in first and head for our room. You can come up shortly. By the way, I took the liberty of ransacking your London flat. Loaded up your suitcase with a change of clothes and your toiletries."

"Much obliged, Mike. I could use them."

Later they joined up in their room. Preston opened the curtains. "A spectacular view of Lake Zurich. Come on, let's go down to the restaurant and have dinner—and a few drinks. We'll get a corner table, away from everybody. Don't tell Winston."

Preston spent the next hour telling Mike everything that happened, beginning with his encounter with Sabrina at the outdoor café. In the meantime, they enjoyed a fabulous spaghetti dinner and a fine red wine.

"You never seem to amaze me, ol' chap." Mike shook his head. "You're a cat with nine lives. The only problem is you've used up eight."

"No bad vibes, Mike. No bad vibes."

"All right. I'll run you through tomorrow's activities. Michael Gentile, our Italian agent, has discovered that your fat friend Cue is leaving on the three-thirty flight to Salzsburg tomorrow. Michael will contact you when you get to Venice and inform you of Cue's itinerary. In the meantime, you'll be on the same plane as Cue." Mike withdrew an airline ticket from his coat pocket and handed it over.

"No way. Cue will recognize me instantly."

"We're aware of that. Tomorrow morning we'll be on our way to a sweet little gentleman's house not far from here. The man specializes in makeup for local plays and theatre." Mike let out a chuckle. "You'll get a kick out of this fellow, I assure you."

"Dammit, Mike. I hate makeup."

Mike smiled. "We'd better head back to the room and get a good night's sleep. You're going to need it."

The next morning, after a nice breakfast, the two went out for their meeting with the makeup artist, Raphael. "Here, put this wedding ring on," Mike instructed, handing a ring to Preston.

Preston pitched the ring into the air and caught it before putting it on. "Mike, seeing a wedding ring on my finger is about as likely as seeing Queen Elizabeth with a pygmy bone through her nose."

Mike smiled. Living the life they'd chosen, they had little choice in the matter. "The man you're about to meet," he explained, "knows nothing about you other than that your wife is having an affair—and you want to catch her yourself. Clever, huh? No use taking chances."

They arrived at the artist's studio condo, entering through the open side door. "Raphael told me this door would be unlocked; he said to make ourselves comfortable—he might be late."

They both flopped down on the lavender-and-green checked sofa. Preston observed the lavish surrounding décor. Mirrors everywhere reflected the bright pastel colors of the condo. "I hope he does a better job on my face, than he did with this room," Preston said.

Soon a short thin man in his fifties with a thin beard entered the room and greeted them in a drawn-out, feminine voice. "Good morning, gentlemen. Shall we get on with it? I haven't much time." He turned to Preston and introduced himself: "My name is Raphael Salinger. I presume you are the man I'm going to be working on."

"That is correct." Preston didn't offer his name.

"Marvelous, marvelous. Such a handsome face to work on . . . a pity to cover it up." Raphael shuffled over to a nearby chair and motioned for Preston to join him. "Come, come, let us begin." With a sigh of exasperation directed at Mike, he followed Raphael to the makeup table and sat down. Raphael wasted no time getting started; he brushed Preston's hair as he talked. "Such a shame. If I caught my lover with another man, I would just die."

Preston mumbled, "Surely this won't take long?" He glanced at Mike and caught him trying to hold back laughter.

"What did you say, young man?" Raphael streaked shades of deep gray into Preston's hair.

"Nothing, just . . . nothing." Preston replied.

The two agents arrived at the airport two hours later. Preston bade Mike farewell, checked his luggage, and awaited Cue's arrival. As he waited near the security check-in, he tugged at his new thick gray beard. He detested disguises; they seemed so silly. However, he had to admit this one felt like the real thing.

He noticed himself in a nearby mirror. It was a professional job, Preston would give Raphael that, though it was probably a bit overdone. The eyebrows were thick, with touches of gray, and the beard was nearly as gray as the hair. Even inside his ears, small patches of gray poked out. Lines were prominent around his eyes and forehead. Preston grinned at his new outfit—baggy corduroy pants, a checkered shirt, and a yellow cardigan. "My God," he mumbled, "Is this what I am going to look like in a few years? What the hell, I probably won't live that long anyway."

Preston lit a cigarette. The clock on the wall above indicated their boarding time was less than twenty minutes away; Cue was nowhere to be seen. Preston's concern intensified as the passengers lined up to begin boarding. "Dammit," he said. "All this makeup for nothing."

Then, in the distance, he saw Cue moving toward the security checkpoint. Sabrina was with him, and Preston smiled. They were followed by another man Preston hadn't seen before—probably a combination bodyguard and errand boy, judging by his looks. They made quite a threesome: a roly-poly man with a Fu Manchu goatee and a black alligator pool case, a rough-looking bodyguard, and Sabrina, a woman of breathtaking beauty.

Her yellow paisley dress flowed about her as if it were made from butterfly wings. She and the bodyguard passed quickly through security. Cue requested a hand pat-down, claiming he was superstitious—he told the guard that every time he checked his pool case, he lost a tournament. The Colonel had briefed Preston on Cue's peculiar routines.

Airline security allowed the hand inspection, shrugging it off as a harmless idiosyncrasy of Cue's.

Preston recalled a story Winston had told him about Cue's airport adventures. Two years ago, a security supervisor at the Las Vegas airport had been sked by the FBI to diligently search Cue's pool case and run it through the X-ray apparatus. When Cue arrived he did just that, thoroughly examining the pool case, looking for contraband hidden in hollow parts of the case and disassembling the pool cue. The effort proved futile; they found nothing. Embarrassed, the security agent had apologized to Cue, who just shrugged it off with a laugh. "You were just doing your job," he said.

The FBI later related the incident to Winston. "Clever little fox, isn't he?" Winston was sure Cue had been tipped off in advance by a loyal security guard he'd done favors for in the past, and he'd simply put a normal pool cue in the alligator case.

Preston watched the trio board the plane. He followed them at a distance, passing them as he made his way through the first-class section. Sabrina, sitting in the aisle seat, bumped Preston's leg with her elbow as he passed by.

"Oh, excuse me," she said. "I'm so sorry."

Making no eye contact, he nodded his head and continued down the aisle, sitting next to an attractive woman—he guessed she was in her early thirties. After a brief conversation, Preston discovered she owned her own modeling agency in Paris. Preston's flirting soon faded when he remembered his disguise; he doubted she was excited about being romanced by a man in his seventies. Preston polished off two quick scotches, and took a long nap.

Four hours later, on the outskirts of Venice, he boarded a *vapretto*, a Venetian boat. He instructed the boatman to stay well behind the trio he'd been tailing since they landed in Salzsburg. Concerned they might recognize him as the same person on their flight, Preston put on dark sunglasses and pulled a brown tweed hat down over his eyes. He wore a black windbreaker over the yellow cardigan.

Their water journey began and Preston, no longer forced to devote his attention to tailing the trio, relaxed and lit a cigarette. He propped his legs up on a vacant seat and leaned back against the wooden railing, anticipating the *vaporetto*'s arrival at St. Mark's Square, some thirty minutes away.

Preston studied Venice from his floating vantage point. The famous Grand Canal, which varied in width between 100 and 225 feet, bisected the city. A town blessed with the absence of wheels, one traveled here only by boat or by foot—there were no automobiles, no trucks, and no motorcycles. The only sounds to be heard were voices, the ringing of church bells, the muttered puttering of the *vaporettos*, and the constant presence of waves slapping against the sides of the canals. If it weren't for the tourists and the water buses, one might conclude he was in another century.

As he observed the ancient, dilapidated structures on each side of the Grand Canal, he savored the unique flavor of this remarkable city. Their *vaporetto* made its slow journey through time, dodging an occasional gondola, on its way to St. Mark's Square, the heart of Venice.

Venice was settled some thirteen hundred years ago by inhabitants of the northern Adriatic coast, who had taken refuge in this muddy sanctuary from the barbarian tribes that rampaged through Italy after the fall of the Roman Empire. As time passed, the city grew bigger and sturdier, and stone structures replaced the older, more primitive ones. These buildings had stood the test of time, though the sea had risen to such a precarious level that it had engulfed the first floor of many of these architectural wonders.

The palaces seemed to him like cleverly painted stage backdrops, barely able to withstand the coastal wind. It was eerie to see the gondolas pull up to the ornate churches and palaces, their moss-covered marble steps partly submerged and no longer of use due to the rising sea level. He wondered if Italy would ever be able to prevent the slow drowning of its treasures.

The *vaporetto* docked in the front of the Piazza of St. Mark, the center of the city's action. Not far away was the Doge's Palace, built in 1301 and later rebuilt, off and on, for over two centuries. The palace was constructed around a spacious courtyard and surrounded on two sides by tall colonnades with pointed arches.

Just north of the Doge's Palace was the world-renowned Cathedral of St. Mark, adorned with elaborate ornamentation and a wealth of color. Byzantine in style, it proudly displayed five great oriental domes. The cathedral was first built in the eleventh century, and thereafter century by century, its exquisite beauty was enhanced by new additions, such as columns from the ruins of Mohammedan temples. Mosaics gleamed everywhere, inside and out. A campanile rose high, overlooking all of Venice, and the cathedral's main entrance held four bronze horses that had once stood atop Nero's arch in Rome.

While centuries of history were displayed before him, his attention was focused on the trio who had just departed their *vaporetto* and entered the Hotel Royal Danieli, which overlooked the Grand Canal. He climbed out of the *vaporetto* and strolled through St. Mark's Square in search of his pension, which was somewhere in the area. After wandering around for ten minutes down narrow alleyways, he finally stumbled onto it.

He crossed a narrow stone archway that passed over the Rio di Palazzo canal. A short distance away he saw the notorious Bridge of Sighs, which connected the Doge's Palace to the prisons. Built in 1599, it derived its name from prisoners who would glance at their last taste of freedom before uttering sighs of anguish as they were led to their incarceration.

In the pension, he checked into his small, clean room. He raised the room's only window and looked out. To his right was the narrow stone archway that he had crossed; to his left, not too far away, was the Bridge of Sighs. Farther down, he could see the Hotel Royal Danieli and the Grand Canal. He sat on the small bed, lit a cigarette, and removed his disguise and shoes, leaning back on the pillows. Minutes later he decided to get a little rest before his meeting with Michael Gentile, the Italian agent assigned to assist him.

Preston slept for two hours before being awakened by a knock on the door. He opened his eyes as the door opened and in walked Michael Gentile. Michael was about five-nine with pitch black hair—typical, strong Italian features. He was casual in his dress: jeans and a black shirt.

"How the hell are you, Preston?" Michael laid down two large canvas bags bedside the bed. "I brought along a couple of cold Italian beers—have one. With your upcoming adventures, I didn't think you'd want anything stronger. Sorry to wake you." He spoke distinctly, with an Italian accent.

"How do you like this enchanted city?" he asked. "One never grasps the feel for this place until he gets lost in the maze of walkways. Sometimes it takes forever to weave your way back to where you started. It's virtually impossible without guidance from the locals."

Preston nodded. "Yes, I've had a taste of that already."

"To bring you up to date . . ." Michael continued, "This the fourth time in less than a year that Cue has come to Venice. His patterns are predictable, for the most part. One or two nights he stays at the Royal Danieli. In the evenings, he dines out in fine restaurants. After, he strolls through St. Mark's square and along the waterfront back to his hotel. He's usually back by ten. Sometimes Sabrina as joins him, but he always has his bodyguard with him. After he returns to his hotel, at eleven sharp, a gondola arrives at the opening of the Rio de Palazzo canal, and his bodyguard replaces the gondolier. Then the gondola proceeds down the canal under the Bridge of Sighs, passes this window, and continues on down the canal." Michael lit a cigarette. "On several occasions we've attempted to follow him on foot, to no avail. We can only cover him until his gondola enters the dark back canals, where there are no walkways on the sides. And there's no way to follow him on a gondola—it's too obvious."

Michael stopped for a moment, finishing his beer, and continued: "Cue is no fool. He's as cleaver and intelligent as they come. He rarely makes a mistake. His cautiousness almost borders on absurdity."

"He must be related to the Colonel," Preston interjected.

"I think we've figured out a way to follow him this time. We know that he is meeting someone, but we don't know where. It's probably an agent, smuggler, or terrorist— or all three in one." Michael grinned. "That's where you come in. We need to know where, who, and why."

"So I'm the lucky one," Preston said.

"I knew you would be thrilled. Anyway, do you remember when you spent two weeks in extensive scuba training?"

"I do, unfortunately." Preston sighed. "I'm getting the picture now: a nice little evening swim, except this time instead of the crystal blue waters of Bermuda, I'll be wallowing in the filthy canals of Venice."

Michael gave him a sympathetic look. He flopped the two canvas bags onto the bed and began laying the gear out, going over each item with Preston. "Here's the usual wetsuit. One major deviation: the bottoms of the feet are heavily padded, in case you have to do a little walking—or running."

Michael pitched a pair of goggles over to him. "These are equipped with a lightweight periscope that can expand up to thirty inches. You can peek through the periscope while keeping the goggles on."

Preston smiled. "Clever. This must have been the Colonel's idea."

"Here are some fins, which you can remove if you need to run. And one final thing . . ." Michael reached into one of the bags. "Here's your poison-tipped spear gun."

"You can't be serious?"

"Just a little joke." Michael laughed. "But we do have air tanks, very small and quiet, with jets to make your evening swim more enjoyable. Any questions?"

"No."

"Good. Let's get started."

Minutes later, his gear in place, Preston stood by the open window. It was now eleven; his night adventure was about to begin. Pulling a chair to the open window in the pitch dark room, he lit what he knew would be his last cigarette for quite some time—maybe even his last, period. He savored it like a five dollar cigar, inhaling deeply and blowing the smoke out the open window.

Michael paced about the room, restlessly awaiting Cue's arrival in the gondola. "I wish Cue would hurry up," he said. "I hate to wait."

"By the way, Michael," Preston asked. "Why the hell did I have to tail them all day long, when Cue's usual itinerary is well known?"

"Good question," Michael said. "If he suddenly changed courses, or stayed in a different hotel—all would be lost. We would have no way of tracking his activities."

"Good point." Preston smiled. "Now I know why we keep you around." Preston looked down the canal, using a small pair of night-vision binoculars. "You can relax now. There's a gondola floating down the canal, not far from the Bridge of Sighs. Our roly-poly chap is in it."

Cue's gondola passed below their window, continuing past the arch bridge ahead. Cue's hefty bodyguard, the gondolier, looked up at his boss. "I sure hope I don't have to have a physical encounter with that gorilla," Preston said. He leaned out the window, watching the duo float down the narrow canal. Cue, lounging comfortably, chatted with the gondolier and pointed at various architectural outcroppings alongside of the canal. "He's probably boring the guard to death with his knowledge of the canal." Preston said.

He laid his night vision binoculars on the nearby table. "Let's go. They're far enough away now." Preston put on his goggles and placed a magnetic four-inch knife on his right air tank.

"Good luck," said Michael.

"Make sure you have a cigarette and a scotch waiting for me, when I return." Preston threw his leg over the window ledge, looking around to make sure he wouldn't be seen. While Michael held the rope, he descended and entered the canal. Michael pulled the rope back up and gave Preston a high sign. Preston acknowledged with a thumb's up gesture, then dipped down under the water's edge.

He puttered ahead silently, eerily, remaining just below the water level. He knew this first stretch of canals would have to be negotiated with caution to escape detection. He would stay underwater as much as possible, rising up every so often with his night-vision periscope to track the gondola. This would be tricky; these canals were like trails in an ant colony. There was no rhyme or reason to them—they twisted and curved in every direction. If Cue's gondola made a sudden turn, he might miss it. And there was always the possibility of following the wrong gondola. Then all would be lost.

He caught up with Cue, being careful not to get too close. He reduced his speed. Of all the bizarre stunts he'd pulled off in his long career, this beat them all. Who could ever imagine scuba diving around the canals of Venice? He continued to surface every so often to look through the periscope.

The water was so dark and filthy, it was like swimming along the bottom of the Mississippi. Venice was a romantic city for romantic people, but his admiration for the city was being strained. The not-so-romantic person saw Venice as a village of old dilapidated structures, dissected by filthy, odor-filled canals. Creatures of the night were everywhere: rats, rats, and more rats. Stray cats proliferated; they were as much a part of Venice as the gondolas and the *vaporettos*, and they damn sure weren't living on a fish diet—there wasn't a sea creature alive that could survive five minutes in this murk.

Not only were there cats everywhere, but every Venetian owned at least one dog. Big ones, little ones, every breed possible. And every Venetian seemed to join in the daily ritual of walking their muzzled dogs. There were no fields, no meadows, and no parks, in which to walk these furry beasts, nothing but the stone courtyards and walkways of the city. Consequently the pathways were left like concentrated mine fields, awaiting the footsteps of careless tourists. And if one was fortunate enough to avoid these "presents," there were also thousands upon thousands of begging pigeons that would do their best to finish the job. Crews were constantly working to cleanse the city. Every morning, all of this organic matter was hosed away.

A shocking thought crossed his mind: Where does pound after pound of this stuff wind up? Preston couldn't clear this thought from his mind as he puttered through the dark waters. The water seemed thicker now.

Preston followed the gondola through one canal after another, out of the tourist sections and among the vacant and partially dilapidated structures of unseen Venice, where few walkways and bridges existed. It was so dark here that Preston could move quietly with his head above the water, but still remain far enough behind the gondola to avoid detection.

Thirty minutes had elapsed since he'd started. Silly thoughts entered his bored mind as he looked downward. *What the hell is below all that muddy, stench ridden crap? How deep is this canal? How thick is that goop-layer of animal feces?*

Thousands of broken bottles must have accumulated down there over the centuries. And what about the thousands of rats and cats that must have drowned and now lay rotting in this organic junkyard? Or the human bones and skulls that must be down there, swishing back and forth, the result of centuries of intermittent wars and frequent murders.

His imagination was getting the best of him. What would happen if his tanks quit working, and he wasn't strong enough to swim to an area where he could climb out of the canal? Or what if he blacked out, sinking silently down into the decaying waste, spending the last few seconds of his life among the rotting creatures? He gave a watery slap to his cheek. "Come to your senses, chap. We have work to do."

The gondola turned into a narrow canal, and he turned with it. The rendezvous was about to happen; in the distance, another gondola was docked near the edge of a narrow walkway. A man in the other gondola waved a lantern from side to side. The night was cloudy, with no moonlight, the bright lantern was the only light to be seen. This dark section of Venice consisted mostly of dilapidated, empty structures, their windows broken. A few animals—some alive, some dead—were the only inhabitants behind these crumbling bricks. Rats could be seen and heard everywhere, crawling along window ledges, scampering about in dark corners— and a few drowned ones floating in the canal.

Preston could discern four dark figures; one was carrying the lantern. Behind them their exaggerated shadows flickered on the wall. Preston edged closer. Two men stepped off their respective gondolas and entered a nearby building, taking the lantern with them. Everything fell into pitch blackness.

Preston assumed the two men in the building were Cue and his contact. Without being discovered, he had to get close enough to find out the purpose of their rendezvous. It wasn't going to be easy—sneaking past the gondoliers and entering the vacant building without making a sound.

He took a deep breath, turned his jets off, and swam underwater as close as he dared. He could hear the two gondoliers conversing. Raising his head out of the water, he slowly climbed onto the walkway. He removed his fins and goggles and laid them down. Luck was with him tonight: he saw a door beside the walkway, its bottom half mostly missing.

Inside, he could see nothing but a few light rays from the lantern, shining through the wall just ahead of him. He crept closer, scooting his legs slowly forward, careful not to kick any objects on the floor. He had to move with extreme caution, but time was crucial. As he approached, he heard small feet scurrying across the room. Rats, or cats, or both.

Seconds later, he reached the wall There was an opening there, large enough for Preston to observe the two men. Then he stepped on a cat's tail; the animal's shriek echoed through the room. "Dammit," he muttered. Looking down, he saw the cat dart off into the darkness.

He recognized Cue's voice: "What the hell was that? Toski, someone is there." Preston heard a gun cock.

"Probably just another cat in heat," the other man said. "They're everywhere. Such a nuisance."

"I'm not so sure." Cue approached the wall, one hand holding the lantern, the other holding a gun.

Preston crouched on the floor and awaited Cue's approach. Cue held the lantern up to the wall for a few seconds.

"I'm still not convinced," Cue said. "I'm going to scoot this crate over by the wall and stand on it, to get a better look." Preston didn't want to hear those words. If he was detected, he had two choices: jerk the gun out of Cue's hand when he peered in, or make a run for it.

"Sebastian, you're paranoid," Toski said. "There's no way anyone could be over there. The only way to get here is by gondola. We would have seen him in the canal. Come on, dammit, I don't have all night."

Cue relaxed. He walked back over to the wooden table, put the lantern down, and sat on a wooden crate.

Preston, peering through the opening, sighed with relief. Toski was a small, stocky fellow with a thick mustache and bushy eyebrows. His unkempt hair hung below his ears. The way he looked, Preston guessed he was probably Russian or a Bulgarian.

"All right, Sebastian, let's get on with it," Toski ordered.

Cue opened his black alligator pool case and took out both parts of the pool cue. He carefully removed the cue tip, then stuck what appeared to be a long brass needle down into the cue and pulled out a cylinder about three inches long. Popping the top off, he shook the insides onto the table.

Cue smiled as lit up a cigar. "Toski, this is what your organization has been waiting for. There's enough damaging information in this microfilm to set the US Navy back for a *long* time." A sinister grin crossed his face. "Here's everything you ever wanted to know about the US nuclear submarine fleet, but were afraid to ask." Cue laughed at his own humor.

Toski remained silent, emotionless. "Get on with it." He ordered impatiently.

"There's information on everything here: submarine routes, how many subs there are, even a rough blueprint of future designs. Also, most importantly, the names of the CIA agents operating in Bulgaria, as well as six of their agents operating in Russia."

Toski finally showed some emotion. He produced a small leather pouch and poured out several small diamonds onto the table, next to the lantern.

"As we agreed, here is one hundred thousand dollars' worth of two carat diamonds—the finest quality, as requested."

Cue held one of the diamonds up to the lantern, twisting it back and forth. He pulled out a small magnifying glass and placed it in front of his right eye to take a closer look.

"Enough of that," Toski blurted. He picked up the lantern. "I did not inspect your wares. Neither should you feel a need to inspect ours. Mutual trust, my friend—in our respective lines of work, there is no toleration for deceit or trickery. You know that. It is punishable by death."

Cue stood up. "I meant no disrespect. I only wanted to admire their beauty." Cue unscrewed the top of the bottom half of the pool cue, gathered the diamonds, and placed them inside the cue. He took a small scarf from his front pocket and, using the brass needle, stuffed it down the cue as far as possible, to keep the diamonds from rattling. Then he placed the cue back in its case.

"I'll be damned," Preston mumbled. "How many diamonds does he smuggle to the US each year? How much microfilm does he bring back?"

Toski started toward the door. "Let's get the hell out of here, I have much work to accomplish."

Preston hadn't expected this encounter to be of such magnitude. They had assumed that Cue was involved in drug smuggling and art heists, but espionage . . . that had never crossed their mind.

Where was Cue getting his information? All those trips to Las Vegas . . . someone there was supplying him. Then suddenly Preston realized: "Why, it's Bela! Of course. Anything possible to put the screws to the west." Preston shook his head. What he had observed was major. Lives were at risk. This information could be devastating to the free world if something wasn't done immediately.

He retreated to the door he'd entered and peered out of a boarded window. The two men had entered their gondolas and begun their night journeys. After watching them move down the canal, he put on his fins and goggles and entered the canal in pursuit of Toski. Minutes later, the gondolas' paths' split. Toski's veered left, while Cue's continued straight on, heading down the same canal from which it had come. Preston moved forward in pursuit of Toski's gondola, relieved that he could keep his head above the water.

He scolded himself for only bringing a magnetic knife. "Why not a magnetic gun? Wouldn't that have been more practical? *Never be without a firearm.*" Preston had always sworn by this rule. But now, when he needed one the most, he had none. "Oh, hell," he muttered. "I'll have to make do without."

Preston needed a plan, and fast. Checking his night watch, he saw that he had less than twenty minutes of air left in his tanks. That was no good; he wanted to follow Toski into the more populated sections of Venice, where perhaps he could alert a night policeman.

He decided he could wait no longer. There were walkways now, on each side of the canal. This would give him some chance for an escape, if his confrontation with the two men proved a failure. He didn't know if either man carried a gun, but it was almost certain that Toski had one. Hopefully, the gondolier would not.

Preston figured his best chance would be to quietly approach the gondola, remaining underwater and using his periscope as a guide. He would attack Toski from behind, slitting his throat before he had a chance to draw his gun. All would be in vain if the gondolier was carrying a gun. But Preston had to take this chance; there were too many lives at risk. To succeed the plan would have to be executed with upmost precision.

"What the hell," Preston said to himself. "You gotta go some time."

With less than six minutes of air time left in his tanks, he approached the side of the gondola. His periscope stuck out of the water, barely visible. Holding the magnetic knife in his hand, he grabbed the side of the gondola, jumped up, and reached for Toski.

But he was not quick enough. Toski slapped the knife out of his hand and drew a pistol from his coat pocket. Preston lunged forward and grabbed the gun barrel, jerking it out of Toski's hand. The pistol disappeared into the canal.

Preston chopped Toski's right temple and sent him sprawling into the bottom of the gondola. He turned to face the gondolier, but it was too late.

A hard blow from the gondolier's oar struck the top of his head, sending him into the canal. Dazed and semi-conscious, Preston remembered sensing this might happen to him; his suspicions had proven correct.

He sank toward the bottom, oblivious to what was happening, his shoulders slumped. The only signs of life were the bubbles from his shallow breathing. Preston sank deeper, until he rested on the canal's bottom. He lay quietly amid the slime.

Seconds later, his eyes opened. But there was no movement in them.

Preston stared at the bubbles that rose up above him. Still, there was no expression from his face, no movement from his eyes but for an occasional slow blink. He watched the bubbles.

Suddenly they stopped; the air tanks had run their course. There was no more oxygen left. Still dazed, he showed little concern about what was happening to him. But as he ran out of oxygen, he awoke from his semi-conscious state. Thoughts, no matter how disoriented they were, entered his mind. Preston visualized a waterbed filled with slimy thick green water that spewed violently from a large hole in the front of it. Amidst the flow of water were broken bottles, corroded pieces of metal, and rusted swords, skulls and skeleton bones that blew out of the waterbed with tremendous force. He moved his head, attempting to duck the onslaught.

Preston now saw a ceiling fan turning round and round. It had rats crawling up and down the shaft and on the blades—several were slaughtered by the sharp rotating blades, their bloody legs and tails splattering everywhere. He visualized a huge rat coming at him with a four-foot, hairless tail that wrapped around Preston's limp neck, penetrating his skin as if the tail were baling wire. Choking to death, he coughed for air. As the rat began to attack his lifeless prey below, its giant white teeth, four inches in length, bit down on Preston's lower lip, suddenly his lifeless body was resurrected. He jerked his body upward, grabbing what he thought was the rat's hairless tail with both hands and pulling it away from his neck with a powerful force. A spaghetti-like piece of rope that had wrapped around his neck broke into several shredded pieces and harmlessly floating away.

Awakening from his semi-conscious state, he lunged upward, struggling as best he could to reach the surface. Like a drowning feline, he pawed frantically at the water above him. As he swam upward with all his energy, he removed the air tanks. His instinct for survival pushed him beyond normal limits. Still, the end was nowhere to be seen: It could be three feet away or a hundred, there was no way of knowing in the pitch black water. His arms thrust upward as he attempted to surface.

Preston was moments away from passing out. His arms had given out. He felt he could not go any farther. "It's over," he thought to himself. "If only you had been in better shape, exercised a bit more, kept those eight pounds off, and quit smoking those damn cigarettes . . . You dumb bastard."

With one final hurrah, he lunged at the darkened water above him. His hands dug at the water and finally surfaced, with his head soon following. He gasped and inhaled deeply, like a newborn entering the world for the first time. The air that is so often taken for granted was now the most beautiful thing he had ever experienced.

Preston dogpaddled for a minute, trying to regain his breath, his sides screaming in agony. The edge of the canal was only a few feet away, but it might just as well have been the English Channel as far as he was concerned. His body was exhausted. His arms felt like hundred-pound barbells. It took all his strength to paddle over to the edge and pull himself up onto the walkway. He stood for a minute, gasping, panting, and coughing, trying to regain his strength. Removing his fins, he tossed them into the canal with a big heave. "A souvenir from someone you let get away!" he said.

After a couple more minutes, revived by deep breaths of oxygen, he felt much better. His breathing was back to normal. "There's no time to waste," he exclaimed. "I've got to catch up with Toski." He trotted down the walkway, following the canal. He hoped the gondola would still be on it.

He had no idea how long it had been since he was knocked out by Toski's gondolier. "Hell, it could be years." Preston muttered. Fortunately, this back section of Venice had very few side canals that intersected the main canal. He doubted that Toski would be in any great hurry; he'd probably assumed Preston had drowned. Gondolas were slow movers anyway.

He jogged slowly down the stone walkway, occasionally putting on his night-vision goggles to look for Toski down the canal. From time to time, street lamps aided Preston in his pursuit. All that could be heard were dripping water, an occasional barking dog, and the soft pounding of his footsteps.

Preston was tiring; a worried look crossed his face. His pace was much faster than that of a gondola. He should have caught up to them by now. He followed the sharp curve of the canal, hoping to see Toski, but his hopes soon vanished. The gondola was nowhere in sight.

"Damn," he said. "I've lost them. They must have turned off into one of those side canals." Still, he kept trotting down the walkway. Now he could see arched footbridges and more light. He was entering a populated section of Venice, and there were far more street lamps to guide his pursuit. He looked down the lighted canal, and a smile crossed his face. Far in the distance, he could see a black gondola moving slowly down through the water.

"It's got to be Toski," he said. "Who the hell else would be out this late in a gondola?" He continued jogging down the walkway, and soon confirmed that it was indeed their gondola.

"Now what?" he mumbled. He was going to have to come up with some logical plan of attack. He had no way to defend himself. He hoped that was also the case for the men in the gondola. Toski had lost his weapon in their last encounter, but still Preston had no idea if the gondolier was carrying one. He would soon find out.

Fortunately for him, the night grew darker. A deep fog had rolled in, so thick and damp that round rings could be seen encircling the street lamps. As he moved closer to the gondola, Preston saw a rusted pipe, two feet long, lying on the walkway. He picked it up and continuing his pursuit. But the night's fog had grown so intense that he could not make out the gondola until Toski lit his lantern.

"Thank you," he mumbled. He passed the gondola and stopped on the arched footbridge ahead. The gondola approached the walkway, pulling up alongside it. The moment of truth was here. Preston watched the gondolier turn around, as if he were going back to pick something up. Preston ran forward and, before the gondolier had time to react, slammed the rusty pipe across the man's right temple. The blow struck with such force that the pipe flew out of Preston's hand and into the canal. The gondolier, knocked unconscious, fell into the canal.

Preston lost his balance from the violent swing. He landed on his side on the gondola's floor, directly behind Toski. Before he could stand up, Toski climbed out of the gondola and pushed it away from the walkway's edge. He ran across the arched stone bridge and down the other side of the canal. Preston watched his escape. He oared the gondola back to the walkway, climbed out, and followed the escaping villain. Looking ahead, he could see Toski's silhouette, barely discernible in the dense fog.

The pursuit continued down the side of the canal. Their paces slackened as the long chase dragged on. Preston could not seem to gain ground on Toski. Any other time he would have easily caught Toski, but the long night had put him on the brink of exhaustion. "You fat bastard!" Preston hollered loud enough for Toski to hear. "I'll get you yet!"

By now Preston could see that Toski was wearing out; he had slowed down to a brisk trot. Toski approached Venice's largest arched stone bridge: the magnificent Rialto Bridge. Toski strained to walk up the stone steps. When he finally reached the top, he turned to face his pursuer, brandishing a knife he'd pulled from his coat pocket. But before he could get set, Preston dove forward and grabbed his arm. Both men, totally exhausted, struggled like two eighty-year-olds.

The two dark silhouettes tugged back and forth at each other, over and over again. Finally Preston took control, pushing Toski's knife away from his face. They both onto the bridge, struggling for their lives. But Toski proved no match for Preston, who overpowered the stocky man and turned the knife inward until it made a fatal cut across the spy's throat. It was over.

Preston stood up and leaned on the bridge railing. After taking a few deep breaths, he frisked Toski and removed the microfilm and his billfold from his pockets. He pitched the blood-soaked knife into the water. Then he dragged Toski over to the railing and shoved him head first over the edge and into the canal. A loud splash signaled the end of Toski.

"I've enjoyed the evening, Toski," he said. "But I really must be going, better luck next time."

The foggy night was no longer quiet. The sound of barking dogs echoed through the dwellings that bordered the canal. Lights flickered on through windows. "Well, old chap," Preston said to himself, "time to get the hell out of here."

Having no idea where he was, he continued his journey down the walkway. Judging by his surroundings, he guessed that St. Mark's Square and his pension were not too far away. The problem was getting through the twisting matrix of walkways.

He twisted and turned through one alleyway after another, passing tourist shops, bakeries, banks, restaurants, and bars—to the left and up, to the right and down, to the left and down, to the right and up. Just when Preston thought he was close to his destination, he would come to realize he was lost again. Through the early morning, he continued his long journey through the poorly lit passageways.

The whole night's events were starting to show on his face. Being lost was frustrating enough. But he was also hungry, thirsty, and tired—and experiencing a strong nicotine urge. Walking by bakery after bakery, bar after bar, only made it worse. If this was London, he would have broken in and taken his chances: Food, a couple of beers, and few cigarettes would have been worth the consequences. But here, he had no idea what would happen to him.

Moseying down the walkway, the stress and strain began to affect him, and he cursed to himself. "This goddamn alley jungle. I could find my way through a tropical rain forest easier than I can navigate this ant farm." He zigzagged through walkways and alley passages until he entered a large courtyard. Pausing, he sighed in disbelief. He had been here several minutes earlier.

"Dammit." He sat down against a wall. "I give up." He rested his arms on his knees, too tired to walk any more but too hyped up to sleep. He had no idea where the hell he was, and he looked absolutely ridiculous, outfitted in a black wetsuit. Preston raised his head up and stared into the courtyard. "I would give sixteen thousand lire for one lousy cigarette right now," he told himself, ignoring his previous resolution. "I would give fifty thousand lire for a pack of them—any brand would do." He paused, thinking about the offer. "But not menthol."

He turned his attention to a singing voice: a man was heading toward him. The singing grew louder, and soon an older Italian gentleman turned the corner, obviously feeling no pain. His singing stopped as he stared at the man in the funny black outfit.

Preston knew very little Italian; he hoped the man could speak English. "*Mi scusi, parla inglese?*"

"No," the man replied. "*No speaka Inglese.*"

"Great, just great," Preston griped. "And the old man probably quit smoking a week ago." He opened Toski's billfold and pulled out several lire—roughly twenty dollars' worth in US dollars—and waved them in front of the white-haired stranger, who tried to maintain his balance. "*Sigaretta?*" Preston motioned with his hand to his mouth. "*Sigaretta?*"

The man hesitated for a moment, then produced a

pack of cigarettes and offered one to Preston. Preston gave the wad of bills to the man and gestured for him to hand over the pack.

The old man, chattering in Italian, handed the pack to Preston. He accepted the pack, and pantomimed the striking of matches. The man laughed, nodding his head, and produced a small pack of matches.

"*Grazie, molte grazie*." The old gent, excited about his newly acquired wealth, waved goodbye and waltzed away.

Preston sat back down and lit a cigarette, savoring it as if it were his last before facing a firing squad. Two cigarettes later, he considered his next attempt to find his pension. By now, his eyes were so tired he could barely keep them open. A warm bed would be heaven to him. He couldn't afford to doze off and chance getting mugged or being arrested for vagrancy. With no proper identification and no passport, dressed in a silly black wetsuit in the heart of Venice, he would be locked up immediately.

Not only that, he would be arrested as a thief for having someone else's billfold—and what about the microfilmed U. S. nuclear fleet's top secrets? He would be accused of being a spy for sure. "Where is that damn pension?" he moaned. He closed his eyes to rest for just a minute.

Sometime later, Preston felt a kick to his leg. "Get up, get up," a voice with a distinct Italian accent was saying.

"Leave me alone, Michael," Preston mumbled. "Leave me the hell alone." He felt a tug on his shoulder.

"I told you, Michael, not to—" Preston stopped midsentence. Opening his eyes, he saw two *polizia* standing over him.

"We would like to see your passport, please."

"I don't have it with me. I left it at the pension."

"I'm afraid, sir, we must take you to the police station for questioning."

The last thing Preston needed was to be arrested, with no passport and no papers, carrying a murdered man's billfold and microfilmed US top secret information. "Well, this is going to be fun," Preston mused, trying to come up with a logical explanation.

The polizia took him to a police station, were he was led to a small secure room. A lone guard remained in the room with him. Preston asked if he could smoke, and the guard nodded his approval. "Hell," he muttered, "even they allowed me one phone call, I have no idea how to get a hold of Michael." He chain-smoked cigarettes. The guard stared at Preston's wetsuit. "Ballet, old chap," Preston said to him. "Ballet. I'm the world famous ballet dancer, Preston James. Surely you've heard of me?"

The guard expressed no emotion. Preston didn't even know if he understood what he was saying. At this point, he didn't care. He just laid his head on the table and rested.

Minutes later, hearing the door open, Preston raised his head. Michael entered, accompanied by a uniformed officer. Preston jumped up in excitement.

"All's clear." Michael handed Preston a change of clothes. "Get dressed. Let's get the hell out of here before they change their mind." Soon the two were on their way back to his pension, chauffeured by a small police *vaporetto*.

"How did you know?" Preston asked in amazement.

"That's why they pay me the big bucks," Michael retorted. "When you weren't back by four o'clock, I knew you were in trouble. There were several possibilities that could have happened to you: You had been killed; you lay wounded or beat up somewhere; you were wandering about lost; you were being held hostage; you had been injured and ended up in a nearby hospital; *or* you had been arrested. The only two I could act on were, if you were in a hospital or at the police station. I always keep in close with both—they know me well. I knew about your arrest in minutes. By the way, I'll turn over the microfilm to the CIA this afternoon."

"You don't know how glad I am to see you," Preston said. "When we return to the pension, I'll clue you in on the fun of the night's events."

CHAPTER EIGHT

The glowing lights that illuminated the runway at Gatwick airport guided the British Caledonian jet down to a safe landing in heavy rain. Preston smiled. Though it was a wet and cool morning, he was relieved to be in London. Less than twenty-four hours earlier, he'd been sitting in a police station in Venice with no idea what the future would bring. It seemed so long ago now.

He filed out of the jet, picked up his luggage, and waited outside until he was met by a driver in a black BMW. The two drove out of London on the way to a specialized agent-training area, twenty-five miles to the southwest. Preston lit a cigarette, rolled down the window slightly, and stared out at the green countryside. He knew the Colonel was onto something; he had requested Preston's return immediately. The best he could surmise was that Cue must have accepted the proposal: The long-awaited pool match between Dr. Cue and Santa Fe Sam "The Shark" was on. Preston couldn't wait to hear the details. Surely, Cue would allow the match to take place at his castle. But Cue was crafty. He might switch to another location.

An hour later the two men approached the training area. After showing the proper IDs, they entered the high-security complex. Preston was guided by a security guard through a series of narrow hallways until he reached a small room with a pool table in the middle.

"Good afternoon, Preston." The Colonel twisted a pool cue in his hand. "You're just in time for a little nine ball." Preston grinned. This abrupt style was vintage Colonel. He was a workaholic: no social life, no vacations, and since the death of his wife three years ago, he seldom even dated. He did, however, indulge in an occasional round of golf. "By the way, you did a hell of a job on your Venetian assignment." The Colonel spoke in his usual gruff voice, distinct despite the ever-present cigar that hung out from the left side of his mouth.

"Thanks." Compliments were rare coming from the man, not because he was insensitive, but because he was generally so wrapped up in his work that he never remembered to give them.

"Let's get on with it," the Colonel ordered, "I'll bring you up to date. We've heard from Cue; he has accepted the challenge. The letter arrived five days ago." The Colonel handed Preston two letters, then paused to relight his cigar. "To keep you abreast of the situation, read this letter we mailed to Cue six weeks ago."

Preston read the following:

Dr. Cue,

I watched you play in an exhibition match years ago in Las Vegas. You were most impressive—and very humorous. I have never had the honor to meet you or play a match with you. As you probably know, I've been out of the public eye for quite some time. I play only occasional private matches these days, or tournaments where there are no spectators or cameras around. I will be traveling to Europe in August. There, no will know who I am. I would love to stop by your castle for a little green felt entertainment—say, nine ball at two thousand American dollars per game?

If interested, drop me a card,

Santa Fe Sam

P. O. Box 813

Santa Fe, NM

USA

Preston handed the letter back to the Colonel. "Now read Cue's reply," the Colonel said.

Dear Mr. Sam;

Would be most honored to make your acquaintance. I am familiar with your pool expertise, having watched you play in tournaments and exhibition matches, mostly in Las Vegas. You are a legend.

Thursday, June the twelfth, through Saturday, June the fourteenth, are the only days that I can accommodate you. I hope these dates are convenient for you. If not, maybe some other time? Please contact me and I will arrange transportation for you, if needed.

Anxiously awaiting your reply. Always an admirer,

Dr. Sebastian Cue

"We sent a telegram to him two days ago, confirming your arrival on that Thursday," the Colonel explained. "We will contact again him later this week."

"How did you—" Preston began.

"The FBI is working closely with us on this one. The letter to Cue was written by them, and mailed with a Santa Fe postmark. Fortunately for us, Sam has no telephone. He is very reclusive. To play it safe, we used Sam's real box office address in Santa Fe for the return address. Cue's return letter was intercepted at the post office. A local FBI agent notified the postmaster of what was going on." Preston listened intently, amazed at the Colonel's thoroughness.

"We take no chances when dealing with criminal minds of Cue's caliber," the Colonel continued. "It's very difficult to outsmart them. We have to be perfect; one error can be fatal. For that reason our US agent, John Wallace, will pose as Santa Fe Sam and fly from Albuquerque to Dallas, eventually landing in Munich. There, you will replace your stand-in." The Colonel laid the cue on the pool table and continued. "Don't worry, you'll be briefed about his itinerary from start to finish. John will give you a thorough breakdown when you meet in Munich. You'll be updated on everything he did: which hotel he stayed in, where he went, even what the weather was like. Everything. We don't want Cue tricking you with any cute questions about your trip that you can't answer properly. And there will be no chance of tripping you up by crosschecking plane connections." Preston sighed, knowing this was going to be another taxing week, with another damn training camp. "OK, Preston. You know Lawrence over here."

Lawrence was the mastermind behind all of the agency's cute little gadgets; he was a mechanical engineering genius. Preston shook hands with the man who had invented more lifesaving devices for the British Secret Service than everybody else combined.

"We've cooked up a little scheme for you, dear chap." Winston smiled. "You are, no doubt, curious as to how this pool match is going to be played?" The Colonel watched Preston's reaction. "You're pretty good with the pool cue, but not that good." The Colonel delighted in seeing confused looks on his agent's faces. Preston rarely obliged.

"And?"

The Colonel beamed. "As you have learned, Cue is the eighth best pool player in the US. Santa Fe Sam, years ago, enjoyed the same ranking, but since he has limited his tournaments and exhibition matches in recent years, no one knows for sure how good he is. He could be better, he could be worse." The Colonel paused, relighting what was left of his cigar. "Lawrence and I have spent hours trying to formulate a plan to make this encounter look believable. Cue could spot your lack of championship expertise immediately. If he does, all will be lost. We racked our brains to come up with some type of strategy, but to no avail." The Colonel stalled, blowing smoke straight up into the air. Preston knew this gesture; the Colonel was gloating.

"Anyhow, finally over dinner the other night it dawned on me: Playing eight ball, you wouldn't stand a chance. Nine ball is bad, but it will have to do. Our objective is to make this match believable, so that Cue's suspicions are not aroused. So, he's going to do most of the shooting, but we got it fixed where you will still be in the game." The Colonel smiled. "Have I got your undivided attention, Preston?" The Colonel's eyes twinkled.

"Please continue." Preston's curiosity was aroused. His nonchalant appearance had given way to anxiety.

Reading Preston's facial expression, the Colonel smiled and walked over by the pool table, picking up the cue ball. "An ordinary little white ball, wouldn't you say?" The Colonel handed it to Preston.

"I see nothing unusual."

"Lawrence can explain this better than I can."

Lawrence, a good looking man in his late sixties, with solid gray hair and a well-trimmed gray beard, stepped to the table. "The Colonel and I devised a plan whereby these balls would be electronically controlled, enabling them to change direction when programmed to do so." Lawrence took the cue ball from Preston's hand. "Allow me to explain. In the center of each ball there are small magnetic bearings tightly packed together, but subject to electronic signals that can change the balance to such a small degree that it can alter one's shot. Here's how it works." Lawrence tapped his watch. "This is your control center: an ordinary British khaki watch, but it has a sophisticated electronic transmitter inside. A turn of this knob, one click to the right, triggers the mechanism to shift the magnetic bearing to the right. Not to any large degree, but enough to cause Cue to miss his shot; however, it should be used only on table-length bank shots and two- or three-ball combination shots. Any other shot would be too dangerous; Cue could wise up."

Lawrence set up the cue ball and another ball several feet apart. "Let me demonstrate for you, this is a fairly easy across-the-table bank shot; it should pose no problem for a skilled player, don't you agree?"

Preston smiled. "It would pose no problem even for me."

"Try it." Preston make the bank shot.

"Pretty easy shot, isn't it?" Lawrence asked. Preston nodded in agreement.

"Now try it." Lawrence turned his watch a click to the right.

Preston's attempt missed on the edge of the right pocket. "I'll be damned." He exclaimed.

"It will not always produce a miss, particularly if the ball is heading dead center for the pocket. If it did, Cue would know something was wrong. You're going to have to change the direction of the balls when the time is right. Take for instance, this same bank shot. If there had been a ball near that pocket but barely out of the way, a slight deviation of the ball's path would have been enough to graze the ball, causing a missed shot. You'll have opportunities throughout your match to do this. Just make sure they are difficult shots, and that you do it after Cue has run out several balls, leaving you a couple of shots to win the game. Let him win more than you do."

"What do you think of my plan, Preston?" the Colonel asked. "I knew Lawrence would come up with something. He always does."

"Just one thing," Preston asked. "Isn't this like the Aesop fable where the mouse comes up with the clever idea for putting a bell on the troublesome cat so they can hear him when he comes around? The only problem was figuring out how to get the collar on him."

"Brilliant deduction," the Colonel said. "That mouse is going to be you. You have the honor of setting up the pool table the night before. Our basic plan is this: get into Cue's pool room, switch the balls, and get the hell out. During the match, Cue will control most of the shots. The fewer shots you make, the less chance Cue has of suspecting suspicious behavior. The key is not to get into a situation where you have to shoot several shots in a row; one bad miss or slop shot will arouse Cue's suspicion. Your strategy is simple: When he breaks, let him run a few balls out, then at the right moment use the electronic device to cause him to miss a hard shot. If there's no appropriate shot available, let him win and wait for the next opportunity." The Colonel relit what was left of his cigar.

"Then what?" Preston asked skeptically. "This can't go on forever."

"Right you are. After a few games, you'll have a fainting spell. You collapse, falling hard to the floor. You will blame it on your old injury—over time you experience violent, re-occurring headaches and blackouts. Hopefully Cue's hospitality will allow you to stay at the castle for at least one night. You've got to be able to snoop around and see what you can uncover. We've been tipped that something big is being planned in Paris a short time from now, but we have been unable to determine when and where it will occur."

"Why go to all this trouble?" Preston inquired. "Why not do the investigative work when I break in the night before?"

"Too risky. The castle is too large to be roaming around with no idea where to go, not knowing who is present, not even knowing if there are guard dogs inside. This way, hopefully you'll stay in the main guest quarters in the back of the castle, which we've learned is not too far from Cue's bedroom suite."

"One other thing, Winston. How do we know our pool balls will be the same type as the ones we're switching them out for?"

"That one is easy," the Colonel replied. "All the great players use Aramith pool balls, made in Belgium. Enough for today, we'll rejoin back here tomorrow at 10:00." The Colonel paused. "I suggest you enjoy the remainder of the day and evening. For the next several days, you'll be busy as hell."

Preston returned to his London flat, napped and rested, and then walked across the street to the local pub to chat with the locals. He downed five martinis, knowing they would be his last drinks for quite some time.

Shortly before noon the following day, he returned to the security training area. "Good afternoon, Preston" said the Colonel in his usual gruff manner. "Let's get started; there's no time to waste. Lawrence will proceed with the slide presentation. Have a seat."

"My curiosity is more than aroused," Preston replied.

The first slide appeared on the screen: a frontal view of Cue's castle. Lawrence pointed at the screen with a pool cue. "As you can tell, these huge iron locked gates are the entrance. The castle is encircled by a ten-foot stone wall. Slightly above and behind it is a short electrified circuit that also encircles the castle grounds, awaiting unsuspecting trespassers. Inside the wall, as you can see on the screen, is a thirty-foot wide moat that also encircles the castle." Lawrence paused for a few seconds and then continued the slide presentation. "As you can see by this aerial view, there are gardens inside the moat—except at the back of the castle, where there are only the moat and the electrified stone wall." Lawrence showed the back of the castle, mostly hidden from public view, and encircled only by the moat and stone wall. There were no grounds around it, only small bushes touching the wall of the castle.

As you can observe by the following slide, another aerial view, on the second floor there is a gable that extends out from the castle. This is Cue's little, shall we say, 'hay loft?' Inside is a room that contains only a pool table, surrounded by walls lavishly decorated with photos and pool trophies. This is his hideaway, far removed from the other parts of the castle and only accessible by a winding staircase. Through his stained-glass windows, which he opens from time to time, we've observed him shooting pool late into the night, often by himself, but sometimes with Sabrina. He also sometimes sits out on the balcony, savoring a cigar and a glass of wine."

"Interesting," Preston mused.

"Now, this balcony overlooks the moat, the electrified stone wall, and beyond that a two-hundred-foot-deep, seventy-five-foot-wide crevasse that carries a small stream of water." Lawrence snapped several more slides onto the projector screen. "As you can see, beyond the crevasse there's a very small mountain, mostly composed of rocks, many of them jagged and protruding." Lawrence pointed at the slides with his pool cue. "On the side of the mountain, facing the castle's back side, there's a very steep cliff that falls almost straight down for nearly a hundred feet."

Preston lit a cigarette. "So what's the mission?"

"Glad you asked," the Colonel interjected. "It's very simple. Eight days from now, on the night before your pool match with Cue, you will approach the mountain, at a predetermined spot that. You will hide your car and hike up the rocky trail that leads to the top. There you will approach the steep cliff that faces Cue's balcony and rappel down it some one-hundred feet. There you will find a small, flat area almost directly across from Cue's balcony. Lawrence you take over from here."

Lawrence laid out two unusual looking objects on the table, then handed Preston a crossbow-looking weapon.

"What the hell is this?" Preston asked.

Lawrence pointed to a metal box, about the size of a portable typewriter. Allow me to continue," He opened a small window in the box and pulled out a six-inch metal arrow attached to a metal cable. He took the crossbow and laid it next to the metal box. "Watch carefully," he said. "This arrow will be loaded onto the crossbow, with the metal cable wrapping around the side." Lawrence opened up a tube on the crossbow's side, placed the cable into it, and then closed it. "You will get situated in a military firing position. When you've taken dead aim at the gable, just below the balcony' edge, hold this handle as tight as you can on a hard surface—and fire. Whatever you do, you must hold the crossbow down where it won't move, in order to keep the arrow on its intended path. We will fully demonstrate this to you later. The arrow and the attached cable will find the gable at nearly sixty miles an hour, reaching their intended target in seconds."

"I'll be damned," said Preston.

"Our man in Switzerland is here now. He's been working on this mission for quite some time, and he has already measured the approximate distance you will be firing. There's just enough cable to get the job done, with a few feet to spare. The cable is carefully coiled inside this metal box. Another absolute must—or the attempt will fail: You *have to* anchor the metal box securely, or the arrow and cable will venture off target. As you can see, there are two small hooks on each side, and we will provide you with these lightweight but sturdy aluminum chains of various lengths. You'll need to set the metal box against some rock, hook the aluminum chains to the box, and wrap them tightly around the rock so that the box will not move around. If you don't do it right, then the arrow and cable will miss their target."

Preston just smiled. "This will be a piece of cake."

"Let's remain serious, Preston," the Colonel said.

Lawrence continued: "Unfortunately, once the box is secured, your night is just about to begin. By now, the time will be way after midnight. If there is no light coming from the pool room, you will proceed. First, using this switch on the box, you will tighten the cable until there is no slack. Then you'll attach this lightweight aluminum pulley to the cable." Lawrence showed the pulley to Preston. "Now the fun begins. Your load won't be as heavy, since you will not have to carry the second backpack with the heavy metal box, chains, and crossbow in it. You'll slide down the cable—

quietly and *slowly*—until you reach the balcony, which you will carefully climb. There's one problem, however." Lawrence paused, a worried look on his face.

"And what would that be?"

"If there is stone behind the gable's wooden exterior, the arrow might not penetrate as deeply as planned. There's a chance it could break loose, swinging you through the air like Tarzan. If the arrow breaks loose on the start of your descent, you would fall down into the crevasse, to meet a horrible death."

"Well, that's nice to know," Preston said.

"*Or* if it snaps off later, you could either crash into the electrified fence or fall into the moat. Either way, you will certainly alert security. Hopefully that will not happen."

"Hopefully."

Lawrence picked up a small device from the table. "If everything goes as planned," he said, "and you're able to switch the pool balls without being detected, upon your exit you'll reach down and wrap this delayed charge around the end of the arrow, which should still be attached to the cable. Then, you'll proceed back to where you began. Traversing the cable won't be as easy this time."

"Imagine that." Preston sounded a little annoyed.

"There's a chance the cable could sag slightly, which would not present a problem unless it touches the electrified circuit. And there is still a chance the arrow did not penetrate far enough into the gable. If neither one of these disasters happens, then you will use the pulley until the cable sags. Then you'll have to climb the cable using only your hands until you reach the flat ledge. You will flip this switch on the secured box, which turns the small motor inside. The cable will recoil with tremendous force. When the cable disconnects, it will snap back—again, there are two risks. You must miss the electrified circuit below, and you must protect yourself from the whiplash of the incoming cable."

"Is that all there is to it?" Preston asked.

"After the cable has coiled back into the metal box, all you have to do is hide the metal container and the crossbow where they can't be seen from a distance. One of our men will pick it up later. Then, you'll rappel up the cliff, hike back to your car, and be on your merry way."

Preston smiled. "I think the first moon landing was much easier. Why didn't we have Cue arrested for espionage activities in Venice?'

"We wouldn't have a chance in hell of extraditing Switzerland's pool-playing celebrity millionaire." The Colonel paused. "It would take years."

"You're probably right," Preston said reluctantly. A young gentleman entered the room.

"Preston, I want you to meet William Corbin," the

Colonel said. "He's our man of action around here, the best we've ever had."

"How do you do, William," Preston said.

"Just call me Bill. I've heard much about you, Preston. For the next few days, I'll be your instructor. We have simulated—to a very accurate degree—what you will attempt to accomplish: rappelling down the steep cliff, securing the metal container, firing the crossbow, and crossing along the cable until you've reached the gable, then crossing the cable again on your return. The exact distances have been premeasured through investigative work from our man Hans in Germany. I have made countless dry runs, all of them successful." Bill paused for a second, "Our man, Lawrence, is a technical genius."

"Thank you," Lawrence said.

"We've constructed a makeshift replica: On one end there's the gable, and on the other, the mountain's flat ledge. I'll demonstrate all of this for you tomorrow, from start to finish. You'll make repeated attempts until you have perfected it to a tee." Bill paused. "Any questions?"

"Bill, it sounds like you are doing a wonderful job," Preston said. Perhaps we need to send you on this assignment."

"All right," the Colonel interjected. "Let's get serious. After tomorrow's training sessions, we'll refresh your memory on your Las Vegas training courses. We will make sure that you know everything that you need to know about Santa Fe Sam, from day one: where he lives, who his family is, what major tournaments he's entered, which ones he won, and so forth." The Colonel puffed hard on his cigar. "Everything you always wanted to know about Santa Fe Sam, but were afraid to ask. We can't take the chance on Cue tripping you up with trick questions that you can't answer. You'll even be coached by a voice specialist, to make your New Mexico accent believable. You will be fitted in several Western outfits: Stetson hat, fancy ostrich boots, turquoise and silver bolos." The Colonel had a big grin across his face. "And to top it off, we've duplicated a big, ostentatious silver belt buckle, like the one Sam was presented with when he won the 1976 US Open nine-ball championship.

Preston sighed. "I just can't wait to look like John Wayne in one of his early Westerns. Do I need to roll up my jeans too?'

"No, you don't," the Colonel growled. "But you need to roll up your sleeves and get back to reading the brief we gave you in Las Vegas a while back."

Days later, after a tedious but successful training course, two tiring plane flights, and a long car ride, Preston caught sight of Cue's castle, miles away on the mountain. He carried two backpacks: One contained the crossbow and the heavy metal box containing the coiled metal cable. The other bag contained the pool balls, a small flashlight, the delayed charge, night vision binoculars, a small knife, a lock pick, bandages if needed, and his Beretta.

Hans had loaned Preston his black Mercedes, tricked out with all kinds of fun little gadgets, and Preston now negotiated the treacherous mountain road that overlooked a large narrow lake. He was less than ten minutes away from reaching the turnoff he'd been instructed to take. He wondered if Sabrina was going to be there tomorrow; Preston hadn't seen her since their rendezvous in Venice, some time ago. Had she wised up and left the relationship?

He shifted to a lower gear to handle a steep climb ahead. Soon he arrived at his destination and hid the car in a small grove of trees. He put the heavy backpack on his shoulders and, flashlight in hand, began the twenty minute hike up the rocky trail. When he reached the top, he turned off his flashlight and stopped to catch his breath. "Damn cigarettes," he griped. "When are you going to quit those nasty things?"

He approached the cliff, knelt down, and surveyed the castle, the grounds, the moat, and the stone wall with his night vision binoculars. "Good," he muttered. "No activity or lights anywhere." After securing the rope, he lowered it to the ledge below and climbed down. Removing his gloves, he took off the heavy backpack and laid it down, then reached into the other backpack, pulled out a cigarette and a lighter, sat down behind a small boulder, and lit the cigarette. He took several deep drags, contemplating what he would do next. In the darkness, he was near invisible: black pants, a black turtleneck, and lightweight black tennis shoes, specially designed for traction.

He secured the metal box tightly to a rock nearly and positioned his crossbow on a flat stone in front of it. As he'd been instructed, he pulled the metal arrow and cable from the box and loaded them into the crossbow. He studied the gable in front of him with his binoculars.

"Well, Sabrina," Preston said, "Here goes. Wish me luck." Holding the cross bow tightly, he fired the arrow. The cable unfurled then stopped. Looking through his binoculars, he could see that it had penetrated the wooden gable. How far in it had gone, he had no idea.

Preston had heard the *shink* of the arrow striking the gable; he just hoped nobody else had. The guard dogs barked for a second or two, but soon quieted down. Preston nervously waited for fifteen minutes. Seeing no lights or activity, he assumed no one had heard the noise. He flipped a switch on the box that would crank the sagging cable as taut as a tightrope. "Damn good work, Lawrence and Bill," he said. It had only been necessary to recoil five feet of cable. He attached the pulley to the cable, climbed down to the edge of the ledge, and put on his gloves and backpack. The he grabbed the pulley and started his descent, suddenly feeling like Tarzan. "Here we go, Jane," he mumbled.

Preston slowly descended over the deep crevasse,

the stone fence, and the moat, until he touched the wooden gable just below the balcony's floor. "So far, so good," he whispered. He climbed carefully over the balcony's edge and walked toward the magnificent leaded glass doors. He pulled a lock pick from his right pocket, but before he employed it, he turned the door latch out of curiosity. To his surprise, it opened. He surmised there was no need to keep it locked; after all; who the hell would be entering the room from outside? With his Beretta tucked into his belt, he looked around with his flashlight. He wasn't too concerned that anyone would notice the light, not at this time of night, with no rooms or hallways nearby, and only the long, winding staircase outside. Inside, he could see the pool table. There was nothing around it but walls that displayed trophies and framed photographs.

Everything was going as planned. He switched out the pool balls, making sure that they were in the exact position as before. Then he turned his flashlight off and muttered, "Let's get the hell out of here." But before he could leave, he heard footsteps coming up the stairs. A light came on, shining through the small opening of the hallway door.

"Dammit," Preston moaned. Nobody could have heard him. No way. But who the hell would be making his way up to the game room in the middle of the night? His eyes darted back and forth as he tried to figure out what to do. It was too risky to go through the lead glass doors; there was too much chance he could be heard. He hid behind the tall, drawn drapes behind the doors. The hallway door opened, and a light switch flipped on. Preston drew his Beretta, hoping he wouldn't have to use it. He listened to someone walk around quietly.

Who was this? Why were they being so damn quiet? Had they heard him? Perhaps the room had a security system. Surely not, he thought. He waited impatiently, expecting the worst, frustrated that he couldn't see what was going on. Finally, to his relief, he heard the sound of balls being racked. It had to be Cue, probably suffering from insomnia.

Preston wanted to peek around the drapes, but he had to wait until Cue started the break. He waited impatiently for the sound of the balls cracking. Preston knew then that, whoever it was, their back would be facing the drapes. He waited . . . and still no break. He always felt so uncomfortable in situations like this. He feared a sudden case of the hiccups or an uncontrollable sneeze—silly thoughts, but these things happen. He continued to wait. Still no break.

"Dammit, come on," he sighed. "What's keeping you?" His patience was running thin. Then, to his relief, he heard the sound of the pool balls crashing together. He peered around the drapes. It was Cue all right, dressed in a red paisley smoking jacket.

How long was this bastard going to indulge in the practice session? Was Preston going to be forced to hide behind these drapes all night? "Not a bad break, uh, Sam?

Vintage Cue." Cue smirked. "Four ball in the right corner." Preston watched the ball fall into the right corner pocket. "Five ball in the side pocket." He watched another ball fall.

"You ego freak," Preston mumbled. "You know you don't have to call your shots in nine ball."

Cue laughed. "Sam, by the time I get through with you, you're going to wish that accident had ruined your hands instead of your face." Now Cue lectured himself: "Sebastian, be nice to Scarface. He can't help it if he has inferior talent."

Preston smiled. "So this is our little celebrity angel?'

Cue continued his shots: "Six ball in the left corner pocket."

"Always the gentleman in public, aren't you, Cue?" Preston said to himself. "But I know your little secret now, don't I? You're a narcissist. A power freak." He'd begun to wonder if Cue was all there.

For the next thirty minutes, Cue racked and played game after game, jabbering to his imaginary challenger. The insults grew more intense, the nastiness more grotesque; a good thumping tomorrow wasn't enough to satisfy his ego— he wanted to humiliate his challenger.

"A real nutcase we've got here," Preston surmised. "A bona fide wacko."

Cue finally stopped and let out another obnoxious

laugh. Laying the pool cue down, he said: "Sam, I throw little fish back into the pond. Particularly deformed minnows like you." Then he headed for the door, turned out the light, and descended the stairs.

Preston sighed. Thank God Cue hadn't gone out onto the balcony to take a few puffs from his cigar; he would have seen the cable for sure. Preston waited five minutes then left the room and prepared for his final task: returning to where he started from. He set the delayed charge and began his final trek across the cable back to the ledge.

It wasn't as easy this time, the cable was slightly uphill from the balcony, and it was beginning to sag slightly. Halfway there, Preston was forced to stop using the cable, and grapple with his hands: left hand first, then the right hand, keeping the pulley in front of him. Preston refused to look down at the crevasse below, hurrying until he finally reached the ledge, where he crawled up onto the flat surface and, as he unhooked the pulley from the cable, gave a big sigh of relief.

His hands were incredibly sore; he felt lucky to have had gloves on. With no time to waste, he approached the metal container and waited for the delayed charge to take effect. With his hand on the recoil switch, he waited nervously for the charge to burn out. He could see it smoldering by the gable. When he saw the sparks stop, he immediately flipped the recoil switch.

Nestling down behind a boulder, he waited nervously

for the outcome, watching through his night vision binoculars. And then it happened: the cable snapped from the gable, flying through the air like a lion tamer's whip. It coiled back toward the ledge, swirling and moving up and down. Then, it suddenly jerked downward and grazed the electrified circuit, setting off a blaring security alarm. Then, moving at a faster and straighter pace, it side winded until it finally coiled back to its origin. The cable winder box sucked it in with a loud *snap*—a much louder *snap* than Preston wanted to hear. But it didn't matter; the security alarm screamed out in the night, and the Doberman dogs barked ferociously. Outdoor floodlights flashed on, and several windows in the castle lit up.

Preston prepared for the worse. He unhooked the winder box and hid it behind the boulder, next to the crossbow. The only visual evidence that might be discovered was the rope that dangled from the cliff. Fortunately, it was the same color as the cliff. Preston, with a weak grin, whispered, "Lawrence, you genius. You plan everything to the absolute smallest degree."

Peeking around the boulder with his binoculars, he turned his attention to the castle's activity. He observed Cue and Bela, standing at the edge of the balcony and looking out over the crevasse. Bela shined a spotlight down along the moat, and then along the stone wall and onto each side of the crevasse. Not finding anything unusual, he turned the spotlight toward the mountain, shining it on every part of the ledge, then up the steep cliff, and to the top. After a few seconds he repeated his motions. Then the spotlight was turned off.

"Let's get some sleep, Bela," he heard Cue say. "It was probably just another damn raccoon crawling along the wall. I've got a big day tomorrow."

They went back in, and soon all lights in the castle were turned off. The outdoor floodlights, however, remained on. Preston relaxed, lit up a cigarette, and leaned against the cliff, breathing a sigh of relief that the climbing rope had escaped Bela's attention. He took the small bag of pool balls and put them into his backpack, along with the metal container and the crossbow, and placed them behind two rocks out of view; they would be picked up later by one of the agents.

Finishing his cigarette, he looked at the castle again. No signs of activity. He climbed up the rope, pulled it up behind him, and put it in his backpack. Then he started his hike down the mountain.

Taking no chances, this time he didn't use a flashlight. As a result, it took Preston fifteen minutes longer coming down than it did going up.

He finally reached his car and hopped in. There was no time to waste: Cue's guards could be driving around, investigating the alarm. He slowly drove down the dirt road with his headlights off until he reached the mountain road.

He drove very slowly for several miles, negotiating hairpin turns, still with no headlights. Fortunately, there was some moonlight to guide the car along the road. But soon the moon went behind the clouds, and soft drops of rain began to splatter on the windshield, forcing Preston to turn on his headlights.

For nearly an hour, Preston travelled this deserted mountain road. The black Mercedes shined its long, narrow beams down the dark valley road, like twin lighthouse beacons searching for lost ships. But on this still, rainy night, there were no ships: not a single car had come Preston's way since his journey began.

To fight boredom, Preston reviewed his training: how to operate the electronic mechanism in his British watch, when to use it, and when not to. And, most importantly, he had to handle Cue properly. The Colonel had reminded him: "Remember, you are not Preston James. So forget your sarcasm and cynical humor. You are just an ol' down-to-earth cowboy who happens to be one hell of a pool player."

He was lectured over and over again that Cue must be pampered and admired. Assuming there was no one following him, Preston relaxed and cracked the window— only slightly, because of the light rain. He lit a cigarette. His first mission had been a success; the only failure had been when the cable grazed the electrical circuit on top of the stone wall. But even that had proven to be no big deal. Tomorrow evening, the real fun would begin: Preston's head-to-head encounter with Cue. He wondered whether he would be able to pull it all off, and more importantly, if he could discover what Bela and Cue were up to.

He couldn't wait to return to the hotel in Zurich and get a few hours' rest. He cracked a smile and muttered to himself: "Cue, you're going to learn just how good this minnow really is."

Fast-moving headlights suddenly came around the curve behind him. Preston eyed the car with concern, thinking that whoever they were, they were damn sure in a hurry to get to where they were going; the car was speeding down a rain-slicked mountain road—not a good sign.

"Damn," Preston said, "just when I thought I was in the clear." He shifted to a lower gear and pressed down on the gas petal, sending his car hurling around the curves ahead. The wheels screeched, hugging the slick road as best they could. At times he came so precariously close to the cliff's edge that he could glimpse down into the black emptiness below.

In the rearview mirror, through the falling rain, he could see the car gaining on him.

"Who the hell is this guy," he said, "some NASCAR driver?" He increased his speed, negotiating each curve with pinpoint accuracy. He couldn't go any faster without driving recklessly. He looked back. Those hideous headlights kept closing in.

He twisted and slid along the wet road, twice almost veering off the steep incline. Those lights, now on high beam, followed him at every turn. Frustrated, he wanted to pull over and fire several rounds through his pursuer's windshield.

Preston was perplexed; his car had all the standard protective devices for ISS agents: oil slick, rear machine guns, smoke screen. But Preston wouldn't put any of them to use, unless it became absolutely necessary. He couldn't risk tipping off Cue that an agent had just left his castle. If they found out, all his effort would be wasted. He had no choice but to speed on, hoping to shake his follower.

The pursuit continued, the two cars weaving up the steep incline. Now Preston approached the sharpest turn yet. The downpour was so heavy, he had difficulty keeping the windshield clear. Squinting and frowning, he tried to see through the wipers. Then he saw another set of headlights coming right at him, not far away.

Preston veered right, the car ahead veered left, Preston veered left, the car ahead veered right. He was seconds away from a deadly collision. He slammed on his brakes, his wheels locking up on the slippery road. The car slid out of control, surging through the driving rain as if it had been shot from a cannon, then fishtailing and smashing through the roadside barrier.

The car dove over the mountain's edge, plummeting toward the dark waters far below.

Preston's survival instinct kicked in: "The ejector, the ejector," he reminded himself. Remembered his training, violently pushed the ejector button. Suddenly the sunroof at the top flipped up and back like a submarine's hatch, and at the same instant the steering wheel vanished into the dashboard. Preston's seat was propelled up and out of the car. He grabbed both sides of his seat, grateful for the seatbelt. A black canister shot into the air above him, and a large black parachute opened and drifted down toward a large lake below.

Preston floated effortlessly down, clinging to the ropes attached to the sides of his bucket seat. With discomfort, he observed the $150,000 Mercedes crash into the rocky shore below, rolling over and over until it disappeared into the lake. Moments later, soaking wet from the falling rain, he made a quiet landing. The lake's water splashed against the sides of a makeshift floating raft that had been released from the car upon its impact with the lake. He wrapped the parachute around the car seat. The makeshift lifeboat was just barely thick enough to keep him above water level. By now, much to his relief, the heavy rain had turned to a soft mist.

"I don't believe this," he mumbled. "A few days ago I'm on a street in Venice in a wetsuit, and now I'm in the middle of a Swiss lake, fully clothed." He laughed. "I wish

I had that wetsuit now." Of all the agents for this to happen to, how ironic that it would be Preston on this raft; he had always ridiculed the ejector seat with the parachute escape as one of the silliest and most impractical gadgets Lawrence had ever come up with. Since its introduction two years ago, it had never been used by any agent—no surprise to anyone.

Calming, he reached into his windbreaker's pocket and took out a semi-wet pack of cigarettes. He fumbled around and dug through the pack until he finally found a cigarette dry enough to light. Pulling out his old Zippo, he lit the cigarette. "Thank goodness," he sighed. Leaning back on the raft, he reviewed the last few minutes. "No way could they have seen me in this dark, rain. They must assume I crashed and burned: zero chance for survival. And by the way, Lawrence, I apologize," he said. "I should have never second-guessed your genius.

He now remembered the homing device, planted in the agent's driver's seat. It would send out an alert of his approximate location. "Thank you again, Lawrence." He took a deep drag from his cigarette. "I take back all the bad things I said about you." With only an hour left before sunrise, Preston frowned. "The rescue team had better show up ASAP, or there was a chance he could be spotted from the mountain road above.

He found another dry cigarette and lit it. "Well, here I am in the middle of a Swiss lake, looking absolutely ridiculous, cold as hell. Why did I choose this profession? I could have been a financial consultant, or a stockbroker, or a guard at Buckingham palace, or even a popcorn vendor at Yankee stadium—but *oh noooo*." He sighed in frustration. "I had to be a hotshot secret agent. Brilliant."

Thirty minutes later, Preston heard the sound of a jet boat speeding toward him. It soon pulled up next to the raft. "Get in, Preston," Mike O'Grady ordered. "We've no time to waste. We're fifteen minutes from daybreak."

Two minutes later, they were off and running. Hans Langer was also in the boat, who quickly compacted the raft.

Mike shook his head in disbelief, laughing. "This is getting to be a habit, rescuing you all the time. The next agent we bring onto our team should be a St. Bernard, don't you think?"

Hans chimed in: "See if I ever loan you my car again."

Preston smiled. "Friends. My very dear friends. I can't be responsible for these fly-by-night operations."

"I hate to give you bad news," Mike said in his strong Irish accent. "But cats don't have twelve lives."

"On a serious note," said Mike, "in less than an hour, we'll set you back at the Baur au Lac hotel for a quick morning nap. And then you're on your merry way to see Rafael again—to get ready for Santa Fe Sam."

"Oh, lovely," Preston said. He lit up another partially dry cigarette. "Just lovely. Maybe Rafael will have another bizarre assignment where he will make me look like the hunchback of Notre Dame." Preston shook his head.

Hans pitched over a dark gray hooded sweat suit, boxers, and dry pair of socks. "Put these on and stand over there by the electric heater. Sorry, I don't have any dry tennis shoes that will fit your feet."

"Much obliged, Hans. But I had sort of grown accustomed to freezing my ass off."

Five hours later, after a nap, Michael and Preston entered the side door of Rafael's residence. Rafael greeted Michael and Preston as they walked in: "Well, goody goody gumdrops!" He wore a yellow leisure suit underneath a hot pink turtleneck.

"Good afternoon, Rafael," Preston shook the man's hand. "We're short on time, so we need to get going." Rafael shuffled over to the makeup table, and studied several eight-by-ten photos of a man's grotesque face. He would be using the photo as a guide to build Preston's appearance.

"Just ghastly," Rafael moaned. "It gives chills. Makes the Phantom of the Opera look like Paul Newman. Doesn't this gentleman know what a plastic surgeon is?"

Preston explained: "Rumor has it, his brother went under the knife and the operation was a failure. He died at the age of forty-two. From that point on, Santa Fe Sam refused any medical help."

"How sad." Rafael shook his head in dismay.

"Let's get on with it." Preston sat down in the same chair he'd occupied just a few days earlier.

"Why are we doing this to your gorgeous face?" Rafael inquired.

"Halloween, Rafael. Halloween." Preston said. "I need a good costume to scare my wife."

"But, Halloween is months away."

"Come on, Rafael, you know the rules," Preston lectured, "No questions." Preston laid his head back on the reclining chair.

"Mr. James, these bags under your eyes . . ." Rafael shuffled backward. "You haven't been taking very good care of yourself lately. Have you been partying too much at night?"

"If you only knew," Preston answered.

Thirty minutes later, Rafael backed away from the makeup table. "You look marvelous. I think this is my best painting yet."

Sitting at the makeup table, Preston had reviewed what he needed to accomplish. The New Mexican accent had to be believable, Santa Fe Sam's history had to be memorized, and the pool shots had to be executed at exactly the right time, or Cue would jump on him like "a duck on a June bug."

Preston changed clothes and reentered the room, wearing ostrich cowboy boots, worn-out jeans, a double-pocket denim shirt, a fancy turquoise bolo, and the worst part: a large four-piece belt buckle. "Ridiculous," Preston moaned. "Cue is going to shudder when he sees my getup." He shook his head. "Here I am, a would-be English gentleman, and I look like Roy Rogers."

Rafael approached. "My-oh-my! Don't you look cute? Did I not do a great job on the right side of your face?" Rafael shook his head. "So grotesque, honey, so grotesque. It gives me the shivers."

"Come on, cutie." Michael laughed. "We need to get going. Thank you Rafael; we'll see you again soon."

An hour later, Preston drove off in his Toyota rent-a-car. Hans followed along as he made the three-hour journey to Cue's castle. Hans would be the lookout, watching any suspicious activity.

The iron gates were much larger than they'd appeared on the projector screen at his training session. The thick iron bars towered ten feet above him. He watched the huge gates split open in the middle, pulling back inward, allowing just enough space for Preston to drive through. Once he was inside they pushed forward, creaking ominously. He had the eerie sensation that he had just entered a penitentiary.

"Hell, I probably have," he griped, lighting up a Marlboro red. "These dame things are too damn strong," he added. An inconvenience he would have to put up with in his role as Santa Fe Sam, the Shark.

Preston drove across the narrow arched bridge over the moat, pulling up next to the front entrance, where a man—by his appearance, Preston guessed he was the butler—approached the car.

"Good evening, sir," the butler said. "Dr. Cue has been anxiously awaiting your arrival. My name is Barrymore; I will be your servant for the evening." Barrymore escorted Preston through the foyer into a large sitting room, where he gestured to a leather wingback chair beside the roaring fire that glowed within the large stone fireplace. "Dr. Cue will be you shortly, sir. May I offer you a beverage?"

Preston answered in his newly learned cowboy drawl: "Just a beer, if you got one." Sitting in the chair next to the roaring fire, he studied the paintings on the walls.

After five minutes spent sipping his Heineken, he began to get curious. Where was Cue? Was this just another one of his tricks, or part of his flamboyant flair for the dramatic: the grand entrance?

"What the hell," he muttered. "I need the rest anyway." He lit another Marlboro and admired the surroundings. The elaborate antique furnishings and oil paintings reminded him of his first visit to Versailles. Preston was not an art connoisseur, but he knew enough about art to realize that the paintings were of the highest quality.

To calm his impatience he walked about the room, admiring the high ceilings. Besides the ubiquitous lighted candles, he found something else peculiar about the room. Something was not fitting into the picture. Then it dawned on him: The oil paintings were all of women. No children, no men, no abstracts or landscapes. Just beautiful women, mostly unclothed.

"How peculiar," Preston said, approaching the fire. Finishing off the last sip of his beer, he studied the oil painting above the mantle. It showed a throng of maidens gathered in a field of flowers—so vivid in color. Preston moved closer, removing his cowboy hat, and leaned forward to examine the painting more closely.

"Sixteenth-century Dutch masterpiece by Van Dyke." Preston turned around to see Cue standing behind him.

"Allow me to elaborate." Cue walked closer to the painting. "This is one of only four oil paintings recently discovered by this virtually unknown artist, who died at the age of thirty-four. Sad to say, no gallery has ever displayed his art. This is his finest; the other three are owned by a private collector in Brussels." Cue paused to relight his cigar. Without glancing at Preston, he continued: "At one time, there were many more. The reclusive Van Dyke was an invalid for most of his life. He attempted to correct his physical inadequacies through his desire to complete the perfect painting. He was never satisfied; consequently, he never made his work available for public viewing. When his farmhouse burned, so, we presume, did one of the greatest personal collections of art ever gathered in one place." Cue shook his head. "Such a tragedy: the world forever robbed of his genius."

Sebastian offered his hand to Preston. "Enough of my lecture. Please forgive my rare disregard for punctuality, I have been unavoidably detained. I'm Sebastian Cue, as you know." He smiled. "And now I finally have the honor of meeting a living legend, Santa Fe Sam, the Shark."

Preston modestly shook Cue's extended hand. "Howdy, Mr. Cue I watched ya play several tournaments several years back. Always wanted to challenge you in a match. Hell, as you might remember, we were about to square off in Chicago"—Preston touched the right side of his face—"until my unfortunate accident happened."

"Yes, I vaguely remember," Cue confirmed. "Many years have passed by since then."

Preston put on his dark sunglasses. "You all will have to excuse my appearance, I ain't much into fancy clothes. I wear the sunglasses because bright lights bother my eyes. And I always wear a hat, 'cause I'm a little bit self-conscious about my scar tissue. Shoulda got it worked on years ago, but I ain't gonna let no doctor hack on me. I ain't no pretty sight no more." He chuckled. "But I never was much of a pretty boy. I can sure play pool, though."

Cue smiled, amused by Sam's manners. "I haven't the slightest doubt about your expertise. Please, no more apologies, we are what we are. Do sit down; Barrymore will bring us drinks and an appetizer or two before we start our evening's entertainment." They chatted for nearly an hour. Preston was careful to let Cue dominate the conversation. The less he said—and the more Cue talked—the better. As anticipated, Cue showed off his knowledge.

"A walking encyclopedia," Preston mumbled. "Is he ever going to shut up?" So far, so good, however—Cue had showed no outward display of suspicion. During their conversation, Preston stressed how impressed he was with Cue's residence, hoping for a tour. But Cue made no such offer.

The best Preston he could manage was a walk down a long narrow hallway to an open brass elevator cage, which the two rode to the next floor. The rickety elevator was not to Preston's liking; he figured the junker was so damn old, it must have come out of Van Dyke's farmhouse before it burned down. Stepping off the elevator, they walked up the narrow spiral staircase that led to the pool room.

"Nice." Preston said. "*Very* nice. Don't see nothin' like this where I'm from." He gestured to the plush red carpet. "Shoot, I might play barefooted."

Cue's right eyebrow raised in disapproval. Cue was seldom fond of his challengers; most were so far below his intelligence level that his patience was tested to the limit. It was a distraction that used to bother Cue, but he'd finally had learned to control it.

Preston knew this about the man, and he felt a vexing temptation to agitate Cue. "Don't do it," he mumbled. "Be graceful and congenial. Hold back. The plan is to lose, to somehow receive an invitation to stay over." He strolled around the room, observing what he couldn't see well last night. The walls were literally covered with photographs and trophies. Important people and celebrities blanketed the walls, many of the photos were autographed.

"Damn, you know all these Hollywood stars?" Preston asked.

Cue ignored the question. "Sam, in consideration of your sensitive eyes, I have kept the lights lower than normal. Is this bright enough for you?"

"Right on the money, Mr. Cue."

"Like the table?" Cue asked. "Many championships, spanning two decades, were played on this table. In fact, Minnesota Fats won his first US championship on this table."

"This table has seen lots of action," Preston replied. "That's for sure."

"Take a few practice shots," Cue said. "I'll be back

in a few minutes." Preston opened his pool case. After putting the cue together, he practiced several breaks. A few minutes later, the door opened. Cue entered first, followed by Barrymore, and then Preston heard the sound of high heels coming up the wooden stairs.

"Surely not Sabrina." His eyes perked. And then she was there before him: Sabrina. She wore a black, low-cut silk evening dress; her appearance was so striking that Preston hardly noticed the emerald necklace she was wearing. "A deliberate attempt to distract me," he mumbled. "Nice try."

Cue approached Preston. "My butler, Barrymore, whom you met earlier, will be by the bar to assist you with drinks." He turned to the dazzling woman behind him. "And now, Sabrina, you have the honor of meeting a legend: Santa Fe Sam."

"How do you do?" She extended her hand. "I've heard so much about you."

Before he could respond, Cue said: "Sam, please meet my companion, Sabrina Tucker. She'll rack for us and keep score."

"Howdy, Miss. Sabrina." Preston tipped his hat slightly. Hoping she wouldn't recognize him. It wouldn't be easy with his makeup, sunglasses, accent, and hat. He gazed at her as she gathered the balls for the first break, revealing a considerable amount of cleavage as she did so.

"Rest your concerns, Sam. She not only knows how

to rack properly, she is also a skilled participant of the sport."

"She's the prettiest racker I've ever seen."

"As we determined earlier," Cue said, "we'll bet two thousand a game, American dollars. There will be a ten minute break at the end of each hour. At the stroke of one, we'll play a final game. Then the night shall end, no exceptions." Cue eyed Sam carefully. "Does this meet your approval?"

"Sounds like a winner to me."

Sebastian shook Preston's hand. "May the best man win. Shall we lag?" After winning the lag, Cue broke the balls. They scattered everywhere, with the two, three, and six ball sinking. Within minutes he'd won four games, irritating Preston with his obnoxious habit of calling his shots, which was not protocol in nine-ball. Things changed in Preston's favor, the next two games, he was able to apply the electronic mechanisms in the balls, causing Cue to miss two long bank shots.

When his last bank shot failed to go in, Cue complained: "There's no way that could have missed, unless this damned table is not level." He regained his composure during the next game, sinking the nine ball with a difficult three-ball combination shot.

"Nice shot, "Preston said.

"Yes, I know," Cue replied. Preston sensed there

could be trouble ahead. Cue was well on his way to winning his fifth game with a not-too-difficult two-ball combination. In most instances, he would make this shot—but not always. This time, it missed. Disgusted, Cue popped his pool cue back and forth nervously between his hands. He knew the next two shots would be a cinch for Sam.

"Barrymore, if ya don't mind," Preston drawled, "another beer for me. Well, I'm a little rusty, Mr. Cue. But I ain't doin' too bad."

"Why, yes," Cue responded. "Close matches always seem to bring out the best in competitors," Cue lit up a cigar. "It reminds me of a match I watched you play years ago in Fort Worth, Texas, against Amarillo 'Slim' during the stock show tournament. I only caught the last hour of your face-off."

Preston said nothing, thinking to himself, "What the hell is he doing? Is he throwing a curve at me? Is this for real, or is he setting me up?" If he denied remembering this tournament, and Cue was telling the truth, then his credibility would be shot. Preston didn't like it, he sensed a trap. But had no choice. "Yep, that was a good one, all right. Quite a pleasure shootin' pool with 'Slim.' I didn't know you were down there for that tournament."

Cue hesitated for a moment, laid down his pool cue, and stared at Preston. "An apt observation, Sam. That's because I wasn't there."

"You weren't?" Preston tried to look confused.

"That is correct, Sam, because there was no such tournament."

Preston, showing no emotion, replied, "You're probably right. Hell, I've played so darn many matches through the years, it's hard to keep up with them. I didn't want to insult you by calling you out. It ain't that big a deal anyhow."

"Not all trappers wear fur coats, do they Sam?" Cue asked "Isn't that one of your Southwestern clichés?" We can refrain from pretending anymore. You're beginning to insult my intelligence."

Preston turned and saw two men enter the room and stand by the open door. He recognized them: The taller one was Cue's gondolier in Venice; the other was Bela. So this is where he's been hiding out, Preston mused.

"Barrymore," Cue said, "bring Sam a hot water towel, so he can remove his disguise." Conceit gleamed in his eyes. "It wasn't difficult to figure out. The last bank shot I missed confirmed my suspicious. I was alerted when I observed you in the sitting parlor. You didn't look right: You walked around in those cowboy boots like a young girl wearing her first pair of high heel shoes. Also, you showed far too much interest in my oil paintings, for an ol' pool shootin' hic cowboy.' You answered all my questions correctly, I'll give you credit there, but you were too good, your memory never slipped—not even once. It was too rehearsed."

Cue walked over to the table and picked up the nine ball. Flipping it back and forth in the air, he continued, "When I raised the level of the light in the room, I knew for sure. The color of the balls was too new. After all, I've used the same pool balls for over four years."

"Shall I continue?" Cue smugly asked.

"By all means, please do." Preston answered in his English accent, wiping his face with the hot bath towel.

"From that point on it, all the pieces fell into place. The disturbances last night, the alarm going off and the ensuing car chase. It finally dawned on me that you had somehow switched the balls last night—quite a feat; you must tell me how you pulled it off. Then, watching my missed bank shots, and the different appearance of the balls, I know it could only be one thing: a control system inside your watch that would alter the movement of the balls. How clever." Cue sipped his martini.

Preston knew it was over. But how had Cue known? Did Sabrina tip him off? His attention turned to Sabrina, who stood next to the bar. She gave Preston a *no I didn't tell him about you* look.

"But we're having such a lovely evening, Sebastian." Preston removed his hat.

"The night is far from over, Mr. James." Cue

instructed Sabrina to rack, using a new set of pool balls. "What would you like to play for?"

"Oh, a beer would be fine with me." Preston couldn't hold back his sarcasm.

"How about your life, Mr. James? Wouldn't that be more sporting?"

"And if I win?" Preston asked skeptically.

"If you win," Cue smiled with a sinister look, "I will personally escort you out the front door. You have my word of honor." Preston didn't believe him. But then again professional pool players generally played with honor. Then Preston remember Bela; there was no way Cue's ruthless brother would let him go.

After winning the lag, Cue sank four balls: the one, the two, the five, and the seven. After three more shots, only the six and the nine remained. But the six was stymied; Cue would have to do a double bank shot to solidly hit it. He did just that, sending both balls flying. But neither dropped. Freakishly, the two balls ended up touching one another, with the six ball directly behind the nine on the back side. It didn't look good for Preston, he would have to hit a hard bank shot, striking the six ball from behind and sending both balls in different directions, hoping to drop something. "Well, Cue." Preston smiled. "A blind hog finds an acorn every once in a while." With that, Preston banked the cue ball, hitting the two adjoining balls hard and scattering them. If one didn't fall, it would be over; both balls would be sitting ducks for Cue. The two balls spread in opposite directions. He watched the nine ball move off the rail and roll toward the opposite end of the table, heading for the right corner pocket. It seemed like an eternity to Preston, the nine ball losing speed as it rolled the full length of the table. And then with one last gasp it fell into the right corner pocket. A smirk crossed Preston's face in obvious pleasure. "As I said before, a blind hog finds an acorn ever now and then."

"So true. But the hog also finds its way to the slaughterhouse now and then."

"Word of honor?" Preston asked.

Cue let out a boisterous laugh. "Oh, come now. Do you think I was able to get this far in life by being honorable? Don't be naïve." Cue walked toward the bar. "Barrymore, another vodka martini. Straight up this time." Then turning to Preston: "And please escort Preston to the guest quarters. He will, I'm sure, need a good night's sleep."

Bernard and Bela led Preston away with guns drawn. When Preston passed by Sabrina, he muttered, "It was so nice to meet you, Sabrina, I's sure that you would be a wonderful person to get to know." Preston could only assume that Sabrina had tipped Cue off. How else would he have known his name? Sabrina managed a weak smile but offered no response. She watched Preston be led down the spiral wooden staircase.

"Not bad," Preston said as he entered the guest quarters. "Which of you two gentlemen are going to tuck me in for the night?" There was no reply from Bela or Bernard. Preston heard the metallic sound of a key locking the double doors behind him. The room was very impressive—first class accommodations all the way. Preston walked over by the four-poster bed, lit a cigarette—"another damn Marlboro red"—and opened the French doors that led to the balcony. Leaning over the balcony, he looked down at the grounds below. Preston knew that Cue wouldn't worry about Preston escaping; even if he safely reached the grounds below, he had to contend with guard dogs, a moat, and an electrified wall.

Later, after removing what was left of his makeup, Preston sat down in the leather wingback chair facing the fireplace. He poured a Scotch from the decanter into a Waterford crystal glass. "Why all the comfort?" Preston wondered. "Is this Cue's way of offering the prisoner his final meal before he is put to death?" He looked at the painting above the fireplace, a watercolor of two women sitting at a French sidewalk café. Every painting in the room consisted of beautiful young women, many partially or fully nude.

"The old lecher." Preston's thoughts turned from the paintings to Cue. "What is he planning to do with me?" After seeing Bela, there was no way he was going to let him go. But then again he has to know the castle is being observed by our agents. The best he could predict was that he would be driven from the castle grounds in his own car. A wreck would be staged, sending him flying down the mountain cliff, far enough to sink into the lake where his car could not be spotted from above.

Preston continued sipped his drink and lit another cigarette. He thought of Sabrina. What was her game? Did she tip Cue off? She had to—how else would Cue know who he really was? Preston shook his head is confusion. Perhaps the encounter in Venice with Bela had tipped him off.

"What the hell, its history now." With that final thought, Preston's exhaustion took over and he fell soundly asleep in front of the fire. Shortly before three, Preston was awakened by the sound of a brass key opening the locked door. The dark silhouette of a woman entered the room...

"I'll be damned." Preston said. "If it isn't Sabrina."

"Are you all right?" Sabrina asked, time turning the gas flame up to make the fire burn brighter. She turned around and kissed Preston softly on the lips. "I don't have time to explain everything, but you must believe me: I did not tell Sebastian about you." Sabrina paced nervously. "He's hard to fool; he finds out everything. I'm almost certain the incident in Venice blew your cover."

Preston lit a cigarette and stared at her. "Do continue."

"I can't stay long, if he catches me in here, well . . ." Sabrina paused. "There's no telling what he will do to me."

"How did you get in here?"

"Barrymore gave me the key earlier. I can trust him not to say anything; suspicious of Sebastian's behavior. I am here to help you. We've got to get you out of this castle." She frowned. "Sebastian will kill you. I know him too well."

"Why the hell are you still hanging around this rogue? Haven't you had enough?"

"Preston, I work for the CIA. I have for over five years. We've been tracking Cue's activities for quite some time, with no success. We know that he or Bela is the middleman for the transfer of classified U. S. documents, but we have never been able to prove it. Even under intense surveillance, we can't figure out where he's getting his information."

Preston couldn't believe it: Sabrina a CIA agent. It had never crossed his mind. "You can't be serious. Why didn't you tell me this before? So all that lovesick crap, and everything else you told me, was just a pack of clever lies?"

"I thought you were an investigator trying to uncover valuable stolen paintings. That's what you told me. Or was that just a clever pack of lies?" Preston smiled sheepishly. "And besides, I was under orders to tell absolutely no one that I was a CIA agent. My actions had to be one-hundred percent clandestine. We were about to nab him in Venice until you fouled everything up by killing the Bulgarian. We were set to grab him as soon as he rendezvoused with his contact."

"So what the hell, do we do?" Preston asked.

"I don't know." Sabrina sighed. "Maybe I can talk Barrymore into giving me a couple of handguns. Preston, I've got to get out of here. I've stayed too long."

"Yes, you have, Sabrina."

Cue suddenly walked through the door, with Bela and Bernard behind him. Extending from his right ear was a small microphone. "It seems the children are not behaving well tonight." Cue smiled, a sinister look crossing his face. "We must take steps to discipline our stray sheep." Cue snapped his fingers and pointed at Sabrina. "Please, Bernard, make sure that this does not happen again." Bela and Bernard escorted Sabrina out of the room. "Mr. James, I would encourage you to get a good night's sleep. You're going to need it tomorrow—and the next day."

"What does he have up his sleeve?" Preston mumbled. "I guess I have two days to find out." Cue left the room, locking the huge doors behind him.

"Damn it, I should have known better," grumbled Preston. "He was listening to our conversation the entire time." What the hell was he going to do with Sabrina now that he knew she was a C.I.A agent spying on his covert operation? Preston sat down by the fire and lit a cigarette. "He'll snuff her out immediately."

The night passed; Preston slept fitfully. Shortly before nine he was awakened by Barrymore, who brought a breakfast tray and coffee. Preston was given his suitcase, which someone had retrieved from his car. "Good morning," Barrymore said. "I hope you rested comfortably." Without answering, Preston opened the suitcase to find his clothes and cigarettes. However, the Beretta that he had so carefully concealed underneath the false bottom was missing.

"Thank you for the breakfast. Knowing Barrymore would not answer his next question, he asked it anyway: "How is Sabrina doing this morning?"

"As I said earlier, I hope you rested comfortably." Barrymore left the room, locking the door from outside.

Preston lit a Marlboro Light. "Thank God. Those reds were about to do me in." He putting more logs on and slept soundly by the fire for four hours, when he was again awakened by Barrymore's entrance. "Good afternoon."

Preston glanced at his watch. "I can't believe it's three o'clock. I guess I was exhausted from a lousy night's sleep."

"Dr. Cue is waiting for you downstairs." Barrymore guided Preston down the stairway toward the castle's back section. Bernard followed them, a short distance behind. The butler approached two double doors and opened them slowly. "Very few guests have been allowed to enter this section of the castle."

"There are probably not too many guests who ever leave this section, either," Preston replied. He was led to a dining area. This section of the castle was even more spectacular than what he'd seen before. On the wall nearby, he noticed a painting of a well-dressed girl sitting in a chair by the seashore: a Renoir. "Barrymore, I know I saw this same painting at the Met a few years ago. How the hell did Cue get a hold of it? I don't recall reading any news about a major art heist at the Metropolitan Museum of Art."

Barrymore smiled. "Mr. James, if you're an art connoisseur, the next couple of hours will be a real experience for you."

"How did he get this one?"

"Please, Mr. James," Barrymore's eyes darted over Preston's shoulder, a reminded that Bernard was not far behind. "We mustn't be late."

Their journey ended at the drawing room, where Sebastian was waiting for them. "Good afternoon, Mr. James," Cue smiled devilishly. "I hope you had a relaxing day."

"Why, yes. All except for the morning tennis session."

Cue laughed. "Barrymore, please offer our honored guest a beverage."

"A Scotch, please," Preston said. "With a splash of soda." Preston looked around the room. It was obvious why Cue kept this back section off limits to almost everyone, including Sabrina. The room was decorated with the finest antique furniture, marble statues, and paintings, most from the eighteenth century. Again, the oil paintings drew most of Preston's attention. Every one displayed beautiful young women, semi-nude or totally nude.

Cue gleamed with pride and withdrew a Cuban cigar from the sterling silver humidor nearby. "Have one, Mr. James. These are the finest hand-rolled cigars made."

"No, thank you," Preston answered. "I'll just stick with my Marlboro Lights."

"Come now, Mr. James. You shouldn't be inhaling those insipid things. You ought to be more conscious of your health. After all, you never know when you might lose it."

Preston smiled. He wouldn't give Cue the pleasure of allowing his taunts to bother him. Instead, he inhaled deeply and blew the smoke toward Bernard, who stood some distance away at the doorway. "Earlier, I thought I was visiting the Metropolitan Museum of Art in New York."

"So you have noticed?'

"But how?" Preston asked.

"One of the finest private collections on earth is here before you, Mr. James. Compliments of the most prestigious galleries in the world." Cue smiled. "You've already observed Renoir's *By the Seashore*, and to your left is one of my favorite Renoir impressions: *Young Girl Bathing*. To your right, compliments of the Prado, I have the *Nude Maja* by Francisco De Goya." Cue's facial eyes opened wider, his voice deepened, his face flushed a bright red. He continued, "From the Uffizi in Florence, above the fireplace, we have *The Three Graces* by Botticelli and *The Venus of Urbino* by Titian. I could go on, Mr. James. I have oil paintings from the National Gallery of London, from the Picture Gallery in Vienna, and from the Rijksmuseum in Amsterdam . . . Twenty-two originals from every great museum in the world, all by the most renown artists of centuries gone by, including one by Rembrandt and one by Vincent Van Gogh." Cue paused to relight his cigar. "But there is one that is waiting for me to rescue her, one that I will cherish the most."

"And which one is that?" Preston asked

Cue smiled. "Da Vinci's *Mona Lisa* is calling for me to rescue her. She will be my next acquisition."

"But how did all of this happen?" Preston lit up another cigarette.

"It wasn't difficult," Cue gloated, "It all started years ago at the Rijksmuseum in Amsterdam. That was an inside job. A bargain price of twenty-five thousand American dollars' worth of drugs produced the painting there." Cue pointed to the north wall. "That painting with the two nude girls bathing in a stream is very old. No one has ever been able to identify the artist. I just happened to love the colors in the painting." Cue motioned to Preston. "Let's sit down by the fire. Barrymore, please bring us another round of drinks." He went on. "After that, there was one more inside job at the Prado in Madrid in 1979. Three beautiful works of art became mine. After that, screening of employees became much more sophisticated, security cameras were literally everywhere: sometimes in full view, but sometimes cleverly hidden. So we had to come up with a new plan."

"And what was that plan?" Preston asked.

"I had for some time a trusted employee by the name of Alger Budel, the finest electronics expert in the German army during World War II. Before his untimely death from heart failure three years ago, he was a conniving genius. Our missions were carefully planned, meticulously executed, and—most importantly—they were all successful. He taught Bela everything he knew; my brother was able to continue the missions. It was so cleverly done," Cue stopped to smirk, "year after year, gullible fools attended these historic museums, parading by these paintings, gawking at them, totally clueless that they were not authentic. No one ever suspected. There was no reason to."

Cue let out a conceited laugh, "You see, Mr. James, I would decide on the paintings—usually one, no more than two—and from which museum. Down in the basement, which you will soon tour after dinner, is an art studio. My longtime acquaintance, Pierre Petain, has been my trusted friend through the years. He is a master at forging art masterpieces, including the frames. At first he did his own paintings; he no doubt would have been one of the best had he not been led astray. I persuaded him to learn to forge the grand masterpieces. It took a while to convince him, but just the sheer ecstasy of seeing these authentic masterpieces almost daily was too much for him. He agreed."

Cue requested that Barrymore bring appetizers and another round of drinks, then he put two more logs on the dying fire. "You have my undivided attention, Sebastian," he said.

"Alger and Bela would shut off all the electricity: no cameras, no lights, and no security alarms. They would deliberately do a forced entry; wearing miner hats with bright lights. In order to make the break-in look like it was done by petty thieves, they would blow up the safe, tossing all valuables into their backpacks. Then they would switch the paintings and hastily make a fast exit. This was done in less than twelve minutes, and always on Sunday mornings, between two and four o'clock. Naturally, when the authorities arrived they were only concerned with what was missing, assuming that the break in was conducted by thieves, not by professional cat burglars, since there were no works of art missing."

Cue leaned back in his chair and puffed hard on his cigar. "Brilliant, Sebastian," Preston said. "Just brilliant."

Cue's ego was on a high, Preston could read it on his face. "It was so easy, so professionally executed: not one suspecting soul." He laughed.

"But, why only paintings of women?" Preston asked.

For the first time that afternoon, Cue's voice changed to a much more serious tone.

"Why? You should be intelligent enough to figure that one out." Cue stared at the oil painting above the fireplace. "To rescue my frustrated ladies from the visual assaults that they had to endure through the years, constantly being gawked at, constantly being lusted over by the lowest forms of humanity. Riffraff. Ignorant peasants who had no business touring these museums. They should be spectators at wrestling matches, where they belong." Preston sighed. What ever happened to good ol' fashion criminals? He lit another cigarette and leaned back in his chair. Cue continued, "I have spared these ladies their nightmarish ordeals—hopelessly distressed, imprisoned for life. Only I could rescue them, and give them the admiration they so richly deserved."

Cue's mood changed from irritation to anger. "I detest your vulgar Western culture, centered on TVs, videos, girly magazines, and other means of pornography. I have risen above your degenerate society. I don't need love affairs with your slutty women." Cue paused, relit his cigar and stared into the fire. "I had such high hopes for Sabrina. She was the epitome of elegance, the personification of culture, the essence of class—an absolute treasure. So intelligent, so beautiful. She conducted herself with such amazing style. She was the closest thing to the women in my paintings, the ideal companion for me. The only woman I have ever tolerated." Cue stalled. "Until her betrayal."

"Do you love her?" Preston inquired.

Cue rudely replied: "Of course not. I will touch no woman, not even Sabrina. The main reason for our companionship was for show—particularly on our travels. It's interesting how much nicer people treat you when you're accompanied by a woman of Sabrina's beauty. Especially airport security, I might add."

Preston didn't comment; it was best to keep quiet and he knew it.

"The women I love are here in my paintings, Mr. James. They are clean, they are virginal, and they are refreshing. Objects for my admiration and mine alone. I don't find it necessary to engage in primitive animal urges like the rest of you." Cue again hesitated then continued. "Enough," Cue corrected himself, appearing disturbed by what he had just elaborated. "Enough. How do you like my mountain hideaway?"

"Most spectacular," Preston said. "I've never seen anything like it."

"Almost every object is this back section found its way out of the most historical places in the world. Chairs, chandeliers, candlesticks, lamps, clocks, and statues: all pieces of history. From the White House to the Vatican, from the Palace of Versailles to the Taj Mahal. The most famous museums, cathedrals, castles, and palaces throughout the world. An egg from the Fabergé collection. A chair from seventeenth-century century Buckingham Palace. Five-hundred-year-old candlesticks from Westminster Abbey."

Cue paused to sip his martini. "For example, that chair you're sitting on at one time supported many a famous seventeenth-century century Frenchman. It's an original furnishing from the Palace of Versailles." Cue tossed the remainder of his cigar into the fireplace, and reached for another. "You see, Mr. James, every man has his price. It's just knowing how much to offer, and to whom. I realized at a very young age that the world, for the most part, consisted of fools that are here on earth to be taken advantage of. Almost every man can be bought, if you know their weakness, whether it be drugs, alcohol, monetary rewards, or the opportunity to make love to beautiful women. Eventually, Bela or I will discover their weakness. There are always measures, mainly blackmail. Everyone has a skeleton or two in his closet: photographs of homosexual behavior, orgies with prostitutes or underage girls, the list goes on and on."

Preston listened intently, surprised at Cue's revelations.

"Your western culture is so corrupt. Greed controls your everyday life. Eventually, we will destroy your inferior capitalistic society—and we will do it from within."

"Why are you so bitter?" Preston asked.

Cue rose up in anger. "Look what you did to my father, a very successful jeweler, on his way to becoming quite wealthy. He worked sometimes seventy hour weeks, until your deliberately planned depression wiped him out. He lost everything he had worked so hard to achieve."

"Deliberately planned depression?" Preston asked.

"The stock market crash in the 1930s made many Eastern families—what you call 'old money'—millions as they cleverly shorted the stock market, knowing in advance what was going to happen. The rest faced financial ruin, unable to support their families. Many resorted to suicide."

Cue's face flushed with anger and resentment. He took a heavy puff from his cigar and blew smoke rings toward the fireplace. "I'll never forget the sad look in my father's face, he was devastated. We kept a close watch on him, fearing that he would take his life. Now do you understand my bitterness?"

"Yes, in some ways. I can honestly say I sympathize with your feelings."

"Ignorant masses, like sheep, comprise most of your Western population. They cannot reason above their 'Rambo' mentality. Not only do they ignore the finer things in life, they wouldn't know what to do with them. So void of culture, so lacking in basic mental skills . . . I find it unacceptable. We must preserve mankind by eliminating this cancer. We will make Adolph Hitler look like Santa Clause before we're through. These ignorant menaces will be exterminated by the millions."

"What exactly is your goal, Sebastian?" Preston lit another cigarette.

"A simple one, indeed, we have started a small worldwide organization to perform the most sophisticated terrorist and espionage activity ever imaginable. Membership will flourish as the US continues to meddle in world affairs, such as your Vietnam fiasco that cost thousands of lives. How about your years of meddling in the Middle East, with zero success except to produce militants determined to take on their Western invaders?"

Cue ordered Barrymore to bring another round of drinks. "All your Yale and Harvard graduates, with their know-it-all mentality, have made it so easy for us. What fools, have they ever taken the time to read a history book? No, they haven't, they are too busy playing polo, and attending high society events and fancy parties. In the meantime Bela and I—through his worldwide drug operations and my diamond smuggling activities—have raised millions of dollars to help bankroll our organization."

Preston broke in: "The FBI, the CIA, and British authorities have long suspected you were involved in espionage activities. How have you managed to escape detection? How are you receiving this information without being caught?"

Cue smirked with pride. "Are we having a press conference?" Then he paused with a sinister laugh. "Oh, why not tell you, if it will satisfy your curiosity." He reached into his coat pocket, pulled out a square pool chalk, and flipped it over to Preston, who looked at it, puzzled. "It's amazing how much microfilm it will contain when it's hollowed out." Cue smirked again. "All those tournaments in Las Vegas were not just entered to prove my pool expertise. I had a very loyal middle man at Caesar's Palace, who was a trusted employee for years. He's been my go-between. At the right time, just before a scheduled match, he lays down several pieces of chalk, all facing upward except one. I pick up the downward-facing one before my playing competitor can do the same." Preston knew another smirk was coming.

"It's so simple, so undetectable, I've had your various undercover agents hang around for hours during tournaments looking for a switch, while others rummage through my hotel room, all my actions secretly filmed, my conversation recorded. All for nothing. Such amateurs—I find them very amusing."

"You are a genius, Sebastian." Preston said, deliberately pampering Cue's ego "While we're at it. You mentioned diamond smuggling. How do you get those through customs and airline security?"

"My, you are a nosy little guest aren't you?" Cue chuckled. "In my thirties I spent six years practicing medicine in Johannesburg, South Africa. Between one third and one half of the world's annual supply of gold originated from the Kimberly and Pretoria fields, producing tremendous wealth. It's not difficult to find hardworking black South Africans who are willing to trade secretly stashed diamonds for cold hard cash, or drugs if necessary. Sometimes I could purchase fine-quality two- to four-carat diamonds for as little as one-thousand American dollars. What a bargain."

"So what do you do with the? You can't get them through customs without being detected—it would be too risky."

"You seem to forget, this is Dr. Sebastian Cue you're dealing with: world-renowned pool player and celebrity. People love me, including airport security. I always take the same plan routes, using the same airports, particularly the small ones." He summoned Barrymore to bring his black crocodile pool case, then withdrew his pool cue, which was in two separate parts. "Nice pool cue, wouldn't you say?"

"Looks that way to me."

"But as you will see, the lower half is hollow on the inside. I can fill it with thousands of dollars' worth of top quality diamonds—beautiful diamonds with no imperfections, the absolute finest."

"Okay," Preston said. "So where do you go from there?"

Cue again gloated. "I never send my pool case through airport screening. I approach the security personal, most of whom I know personally, and request a hand inspection, informing them that sending my pool case through screening has caused me bad luck—in almost every case, I've lost the tournament afterwards. They lap this up, in most cases, like a hungry Labrador retriever. If they resist, then I refuse to board, throwing a temper tantrum. I stomp off. I have cleverly gotten to know most of the airport security personal. They love me, and I'm quick to give them an autographed picture of Jackie Gleason and me shooting pool, personally signed by both of us."

"How did you get to know Gleason?" Preston asked.

"Years back, Jackie and I became good friends, hanging out in all the hot spots in Hollywood, New York, and Las Vegas. One night after both of us had way too much scotch, I challenged Jackie to a pool match, offering him a fair spot. The bet: twenty-thousand dollars in cash if I lost. But if I won, I requested five hundred signed photographs of Jackie and me in front of Caesar's Palace; he could take a full year to sign them all. He gladly accepted the challenge."

"You mentioned the Louvre in Paris. Exactly what are you up to?" Preston didn't know if he would answer this question.

"Mr. James, as you well know, curiosity kills the cat. But in this instance, it's not going to be a cat." Cue laughed. "Let's take a break and freshen up, and we'll meet again for dinner at 6:45."

"Good evening, Mr. James." Cue motioned for Preston to have a seat, not far from another roaring fireplace.

"You will be most impressed with my Chinese chef, Yin. He can't speak a word of any European language. He's in the country illegally, so he doesn't cause any problems for me."

The two dined for over an hour, making polite conversation. Preston couldn't recall having a finer dinner: six pound lobsters split in half with special sauces, and prime rib you could cut with a fork.

Preston lit a cigarette, "Well, you were correct. Your Chinese chef is remarkable. Most satisfying. What are we having tomorrow night?"

"Come, isn't it time for your personal tour of the castle?" For the next hour, Cue guided Preston through room after room, meticulously describing every rare furnishing and priceless oil painting by Renoir, Van Gogh, Rembrandt, da Vinci and others. As always, Bernard followed behind. Then Cue led Preston down the spiral staircase to the basement.

"Here, Mr. James, you will have the honor of meeting Pierre, our master artist and forger. This is where his masterpieces are created." Preston observed a very thin gray-haired man, wearing bifocals.

"How do you do?" Preston offered, "I'm Preston James, Sebastian's dear friend." Pierre just nodded as he made final touches to his new masterpiece.

"Does that look familiar?" Cue smiled.

"Yes. It's Da Vinci's portrait of *Mona Lisa*"

"Come over here, Mr. James. Have a seat in front of the projector screen. Bernard will be the emcee for our feature presentation" Cue motioned Bernard to turn down the lights. "And now for your evening history lesson." Cue picked up a nearby pool cue and pointed it at the screen. "As you can no doubt can see for yourself, this is a photograph of central Paris. Bernard, please a close up of the Louvre museum. We have tried for years to come up with a plan to break in, but there were too many obstacles, too many risks involved. It just couldn't be done."

"Bernard the next slide, please." Cue stood and walked around the room. "Finally our opportunity came along. The expansion of the Louvre has been undertaken recently, and we capitalized on this new tacky development. You see this glass pyramid on the screen? The Egyptians would have been proud. The next series of slides show the Pyramide de Louvre's progress, well on its way to its completion. The construction foreman was our first cousin and was part of our team. It was so easy, not only did we have access to the Louvre museum, we even had a key." Cue smirked as he paced. "Am I boring you, Mr. James?"

"Not at all, Sebastian, I find all this incredibly fascinating. Please go on."

"All these years I have waited for this moment. Soon the grandest, most famous woman in the world will be mine, the painting will be switched, replaced by Pierre's forgery— an exact replica, including the frame." Cue stopped to puff heavily on his cigar. "No one will ever suspect that the *Mona Lisa* they are admiring is a fake.

"Tomorrow morning, shortly before dawn, we will execute our caper. Thanks to Bela's electronic expertise all alarm systems will be disarmed, all cameras will cease to film, and all electricity will be turned off. We estimate that we have twenty minutes to complete the switch."

"Your late father would have been so proud," Preston answered.

"To enhance our chances, we've planned distractions. There will be three explosions, all occurring simultaneously. Smoke will pour from the Sacré-Coeur—that majestic palace overlooking Paris—the Notre Dame Cathedral, and the Arc de Triomphe.

Preston looked shocked. "You can't be serious, Sebastian," he blurted. "You, of all people, desecrating historical landmarks.

"How dare you think such absurd thoughts? Just harmless smoke bombs that Bela planted days ago, totally undetected. It will be an interesting morning as hundreds of Parisians run around in panic."

"What do you have planned for Sabrina?"

"She will soon learn how I handle traitors." Cue laughed. "In our taking of the Louvre tomorrow, you will notice the *Winged Victory* of Samothrace, the famous sculpture of a headless woman with wings. Isn't it a shame that sculptured beauty is headless? Don't you think she would look so much better with a head?" Cue smirked with evil in his eyes. "Sabrina's will do very nicely."

"You're sick, Sebastian." Preston couldn't hold back his anger any longer. "You are not in touch with reality anymore. Your sexual hang-ups have warped your sanity."

"And your tasteless remarks are without foundation. Our evening's entertainment is over. Goodbye, Mr. James. I'm sure you will find the next thirty minutes with Bela and Bernard most entertaining." Cue laughed. "And by the way, your watchdog out there has been taken care of."

Before Bernard and Bela could handcuff Preston. He popped his Khaki watch open and swallowed three small white pills. "Wrong as usual. I won't give you the pleasure of torturing me."

"Bernard, you fool, you were instructed to search him thoroughly." Cue turned to Preston. "Very clever. But it will be your last trick."

"You will never," Preston stopped, gasping for his final breath, "you will never, you will . . ." He wasn't able to complete his sentence. Instead he fell down hard on the floor.

"Bernard, get him out of here," Cue ordered. "Check his pulse first." Bernard walked over to Preston and held his wrist. "There's still a heartbeat, but it's a faint one. What do you want me to do with him?"

"I don't know. We need to get started, we must arrive at the Louvre before dawn." Preston lay motionless on the floor, spit drooling from his open mouth. "We can't leave him here, I don't want Pierre or Yin seeing him."

Bela snapped his fingers, "I've got it." He pointed to the knight's suit of armor that stood in the far corner. "We'll stuff him in and drop him over the balcony, let him sink down to the bottom of the moat. Then we'll deal with him when we return."

Within minutes, Bela and Bernard had put the suit of armor around Preston, including the full helmet, and pitched him over the balcony into the moat. "Good night, Mr. James, pleasant dreams. All right Bernard we need to get the van loaded and get the hell out of here."

As Bela and Bernard returned to the room, Preston's body slowly descended to the bottom of the moat. But just before he reached the bottom his arms jerked up, Preston straightened himself, and was able to stand up on the murky floor, at the same time removing his uncomfortable helmet, and peeked his head above the water level. Taking deep breaths, he shook his head in disbelief. "Here we go again. I don't believe this."

He tugged at the heavy chest plate, finally removing it, then paddled over to the edge of the moat and removed the rest of his knight's armor. "Now I know how Houdini felt. Damn, this water is cold," Preston climbed quietly out of the moat. Lying down below a small hedge, he took in more heavy breaths. He raised up and looked about; there was no one insight, no sound, and no movement. Then he noticed a medium-sized van he assumed was being loaded for the trip to Paris. He watched two men shuffle from the castle entrance to the back of the van. He guessed it was probably Bela and Bernard. On their next trip they carried what Preston feared: a limp body.

"Damn." Preston felt helpless as he watched them load the body into the van. "Cue's already done her in." Getting into the van was his only chance. He continued to crawl behind the hedges until he was very close to the van's back entrance. Now he had to enter the van without being seen and find something to hide behind once he entered.

"At least it will be warm in there," Preston decided. He waited until the two men disappeared toward the castle entrance. Then he dashed across the ground and entered the van, carefully feeling his way along the van's interior wall until he hid behind two large crates, almost to the very back. Just in time, for Preston heard the two men as they walked up the ramp. One of them held a lantern. Preston didn't move.

He heard the door open wider and saw more light shining into the van. Ducking down lower, his head touched the floor, He heard more voices; one of the voices was definitely Cue's. He hollered in German; not only could Preston not see anything, he couldn't understand what was said. Then he heard more objects being loaded onto the van.

One was shoved very close to where Preston was hiding, but nothing happened.

Preston waited, frustrated by his helplessness: He couldn't do anything, he couldn't see anything, and he couldn't understand anything. Finally he heard the van's doors close. Silence and pitch darkness returned. Preston leaned against the van's back wall, sitting in darkness in soaking wet clothes, rubbing his hands together to dry them. He decided to wait until the van departed before searching for Sabrina, who lay somewhere in the van, most likely dead. Ten minutes later, the van's engine started, and their journey began.

He crept around the van's floor. Reaching into his pocket, he pulled out his Zippo. "Come on, don't let me down." Preston tried to draw a flame from the lighter. On his third attempt he was successful. Holding it up, he stood up and leaned on a wooden crate. He moved the lighter around, looking for Sabrina. "Sabrina," Preston whispered softly, "can you hear me?" In the far corner, not far from where he was standing, came a muffled voice. He walked around several crates, hanging onto them for support. Guided by the muffled sound, he probed his hand around a crate until he touched Sabrina's hair and felt the gag in her mouth. Using his Zippo for light, he untied the gag and pulled it out of her mouth.

"Quiet," Preston warned. He kissed her softly on the lips, untying first her hands, then her feet. "Watching your limp body being carried into the van, I thought I had lost you, for sure."

"You thought *you* had lost *me!*" Sabrina put her arms around Preston. "What the hell are you doing alive? Barrymore said you took cyanide pills, and then they threw you into the moat."

"Those three pills I took weren't cyanide or any other poison. They contained a very serious knockout drug— still dangerous as hell—only to be used when there's no other alternative. There's a chance they might cause brain hemorrhaging or bring on a heart attack. Fortunately that did not happen—yet." Preston sat down on the van's floor. "The drug is designed to slow the body's metabolism to an extreme low for a few minutes, like a person who's nearly drowned in freezing water. After that, the effects wear off rapidly. The body can be revived in some cases, but not always." Preston smiled. "I was fortunate they put that armor over me, or they would have noticed my revived breathing."

Preston managed a giggle. "I must say, after three decades in the espionage business, I've never been dragged around a castle in knight's armor. . . . Is you circulation okay? You were bleeding around the ankles,

"I'll be okay," Sabrina answered,

"We can't afford to waste any more time. First we need to find a few things in this van, like a sharp tool or a crowbar. We'll have got to dig our way out somehow, are we'll be history. There's no way we can bust those heavy doors open without being heard. We've also got to find a flashlight, or we'll never get anything accomplished."

After five minutes of searching, Preston discovered several miner's hats in an open crate. He pulled one out and flipped on the light, and a narrow, bright stream shot out of the helmet. Preston shined it all around the van: crates and boxes, mostly. In the far corner he observed a tall, wooden crate anchored to the side of the van.

"If it isn't our little lady, the *Mona Lisa*. If we had time and I knew they wouldn't hear us, I would rip that painting to pieces."

"Barrymore told me what they did to you and what Cue was going to do to me in the Louvre."

"Yes," Preston answered. "He delighted in telling me his plans. The construction foreman, Andreas, will meet them at the Pyramid. After Bela has completed all his tasks, they will quickly enter the Louvre, using a simple key Andreas has made. After doing away with you, they'll switch the paintings and within minutes be on their merry way back to Switzerland. The French authorities will be so distracted by Bela's planted explosions, their focus will be far from the electrical failures at the Louvre."

Preston shook his head. "Actually, it *is* a clever plan. We've got to figure out a way to stop them."

"Maybe Barrymore will call the Swiss authorities," Sabrina said. "I think he's had it with Sebastian. When he overheard Bela bragging about what they had done to you— and what they were planning to do to me—he was furious."

"That's a possibility," Preston said. "But if Cue found out, there's no telling what they would do to him."

With their lighted coal miner's hats on, they continued to search for any instrument that could successfully cut out a hole in the thick wooden sides of the van. "Preston, look what I found!" Sabrina excitedly held up a black jumpsuit. "You can get out of those wet clothes."

"Great," Preston laughed. "I'll be wearing a miner's hat *and* jumpsuit. Fashion at its best." Preston removed his wet clothes, and put the jumpsuit on. "It's nice to feel warm again," he sighed. "We've got to figure a way to tear a hole in the side of this van and jump out. If we can't pull that off, we're in trouble. It leaves us no alternative. When the van stops, you can guarantee Cue, Bela, Bernard, and probably Andreas will be at the back of the van preparing to haul you off. I could probably knock the first one out, but I would be dead by the time I reached his gun." Preston continued, in deep concentration. "Or I could hide undetected, watch them haul you off, then seek help. But by the time anybody arrived it would be too late."

Sabrina frowned. "So what next?"

"Let's keep searching. There has to be something

around here that we can use to chisel away at the van's side wall until we can carve out a hole big enough to crawl through." Preston paused. "But then, if Cue and Bela are following the van instead of leading the way, we're dead. But we have no other choice."

"There's still a chance Barrymore had contacted the Swiss authorities. Maybe the French police will show up."

Preston shook his head. "They'll just assume all of this is someone's wild fantasy: switching out the *Mona Lisa*, cutting a women's head off, and placing it on the *Winged Victory*. They would just laugh it off as another prank call."

For several more minutes Preston and Sabrina carefully rummaged through the boxes and crates. "Pretty clever of Cue, using these lighted hats. We'll arrive shortly before dawn, and it will be dark in the Louvre. These will free up their hands—no flashlights needed."

"Preston." Sabrina spoke softly. "Look what I found." She held up a crowbar.

"Good work," Preston said. "Now let's see if we can do a little wood carving." The two retreated to the back of the van, just in front of the doors.

For the next two hours Preston poked and chiseled at the wooden side, pulling most of the wood splinters back into the van, so they wouldn't be seen if Cue was following behind.

"Hallelujah," Preston smiled. "I see a hard rain falling. Good. Whoever is riding in the cab will have less chance of hearing our activity back here. Plus it will slow their speed on this mountainous road." Preston paused. "If it continues like this, they might be off-target on their rendezvous time, and may have to abort the mission. The van has cut its speed."

"Then what?" Sabrina asked.

"They'll eventually have to stop," Preston said. "For breakfast or gas. If they don't see the hole I've made, we can quietly escape." Preston continued chiseling at the wooden side, by now the hole was the size of a dinner plate. "Damn it," he moaned.

"What's the matter?"

"The rain has stopped." Preston looked through the hole. "And the van's speed has picked up. We're traveling faster than before the rain began. At least we're making progress on opening the hole enough to get the hell out of here."

For another hour Preston hacked at the wood around the hole, carefully peeling off the splintered wood and pitching it over by the doors. He wanted badly to stick his head out and see if Cue was following them, but he couldn't take the chance. By now, the opening was big enough to crawl through, but it needed to be bigger to make their escape easier. He continued chipping away more toward the floor of the van. Even if Cue saw them, they could make a mad dash for the busy street that borders the Seine, just in front of the Louvre. Would Cue take a chance on mowing them down when there could be early morning joggers or even a car or two nearby that could hear the shots? Preston shook his head, "I guess we'll soon find out."

"What's the matter?" Sabrina asked, hearing his mutterings.

"Nothing," Preston answered. "Just thinking out loud." Another hour passed, and Preston had accomplished what he wanted: an opening they could easily crawl out of. Sabrina scooted close beside Preston as they peered out of the hole. "As you can see by the lights, we're entering Paris. My guess is we're thirty minutes from the Louvre, but Cue is arriving fifteen minutes later than scheduled. The sun will be rising by the time we arrive; it won't be total darkness like they had planned for, but the three explosions will be such a major distraction they should easily be able to complete their mission—unless we can pull off some miracle."

Twenty minutes later, Preston whispered: "We just passed the Pont De La Concorde. We're on the Quai des Tuileries bordering the Seine, which means we're just about there."

The van turned a sharp left. As it was slowing to a stop, Preston said, "Let's make a break for it." Both jumped out, landing hard on the ground, only to see Cue's Mercedes pulling up to the right of them.

"Damn it," said Preston. Before they could stand up, Bela and Cue exited the car, pointing guns directly at them.

"Good morning, my little chipmunks." Cue smiled wickedly. By now, Bernard and Andreas had arrived beside Cue. "There's no time to waste; we're running behind schedule. Bernard, get some rope and tie them up—and gag Sabrina. If she makes a sound, slap her with your pistol. Andreas, get the painting. Leave the bubble wrap on until you're ready to make the switch. Bela, keep a gun pointed at Preston's head. If he makes one false move, kill him. Now move it. We need to get out of the public view."

Preston whispered quietly to Sabrina: "Play it cool. I'll come up with something." A minute later Bernard held the painting, Sabrina and Preston were tied up, and Sabrina was gagged.

"Mr. James, you're starting to wear out your welcome," Cue said with a cynical grin. He looked up at the surrounding sky and watched bellows of smoke rise from three different directions—one from Notre Dame cathedral, one from the Arc de Triomphe, and one rising from Sacré-Coeur, the palace on a hilltop above the city.

"Good work, Bela," said Cue. "Just listen to the fire trucks and police cars rushing about. That will keep them busy for a while. Now let's move swiftly."

Andreas, with the painting under his arm, trotted

toward the large glass and metal pyramid, with Bela and Sabrina shortly behind him, followed by Preston, who was guarded by Bernard. Taking up the rear guard was Cue. Seconds later, they entered the entrance to the pyramid. Cue hollered out at Andreas, "What about the night security guards?'

"They have been properly taken care of."

Andreas lead the way through the underground lobby. Soon, they reached the lower entrance to the museum. Andreas pointed to the majestic flight of stairs in front of them. The *Winged Victory* of Samothrace is just past these stairs."

"Hurry," Cue ordered. "We have no time to waste." Seconds later, they reached their destination. Bernard pulled Sabrina next to the headless sculpture. She struggled to break away. "We don't have time for that," Cue barked. "Knock her out." Bernard struck Sabrina in the back of her head, and she fell unconscious against the sculpture.

"Andreas, stand guard," Cue instructed. "This will take less than a minute. Then, run as fast as you can to switch the painting. We'll meet you at the van." Preston leaned against a nearby sculpture and rubbed the rope that tied his hands against the sharp edge of the sculpture. Bernard, not far from him, was distracted by what was about to happen with Sabrina. Cue laughed. "I hope you enjoy the show, Mr. James."

"You are a sicko," Preston answered.

"Now, now," Cue smiled. "You're starting to hurt my feelings." Turning to Bela, he ordered: "Get it done. We need to be on our way." Bela drew a large knife and reached for Sabrina. Just then, several shots echoed through the museum. Andreas fired into the darkness, but the return fire hit him twice. He fell to his knees and scooted to a nearby sculpture, leaving a trail of blood.

"Damn it to hell," Cue cried. "It's got to be the French authorities. Someone tipped them off." Cue motioned to Bela. "Get over to the top of the staircase. Anybody comes up, kill them." Then he turned to Bernard. "Kill Preston, kill Sabrina, then follow me. Let's get the hell out of here. Andreas, cover us," Cue ordered. "Come on, Bela let's move."

Before Bernard could turn around, Preston, who seconds earlier had managed to undo the rope on his hands, lunged at Bernard and wrapped the rope around his neck, pulling it so tight that Bernard dropped his gun. The stranglehold was too much for Bernard. Preston threw him to the floor and picked up his gun. Bernard made one last weak attempt to get at Preston—only to receive two bullets in his chest. He fell hard, crashing into the sculpture and falling to the floor. Preston wanted to check on Sabrina, but there was no time. He hoped Bela hadn't broken her neck with that karate chop. By now, Bela and Cue had disappeared down the long hallway, Preston turned his attention to Andreas, but his worries were over as he watched the man fall dead to the floor just above the stairway.

Preston heard a familiar voice hollering from the bottom of the staircase. ""Preston, are you up there? It's Mike . . . Mike O'Grady."

Preston approached the top of the staircase and shouted: "Get your ass up here! We've got to chase down Cue and Bela before we lose sight of them." Moments later Mike reached the top of the stairs, and the two slapped hands and ran down the hallway.

"What the hell are you doing here?" Preston asked.

"It's a long story," Mike answered.

"Anyhow, damn glad to see you. You just saved Sabrina's life—and mine. We need to figure out where the hell Cue and Bela are."

"There are several exits out of this museum. Who knows which one they're headed for?" They continued running down the long hallway. It was an eerie feeling, running through the most famous museum in the world, no lights on, no tourists, the only sounds their shoes pounding hard on the marble floor. They passed famous old paintings, statues, and sculptures from centuries ago.

"Damn," Preston moaned. "I don't think we can catch up with them." In the distance, they heard four shots fired.

"They're shooting the lock off!" Preston turned right. "This way. Hurry." A minute later, they reached the exit door Cue and Bela had blown open. Outside, they could see the two men approaching a royal blue Mercedes convertible, parked alongside the Seine.

Cue and Bela approached the car, jerking a Japanese woman out of the driver's seat.

Cue pushed the tourist hard into the back seat, "We'll use her for cover." Bela jumped into the driver's seat. Tires screeched as they sped off.

Preston and Mike chased them down the street. A black man in a 1974 Oldsmobile pulled up beside them. "You guys need some help?" he asked.

"Secret Service." Mike pulled out his identification. "We need to borrow your car."

"Right on," the man said. "But I'm coming along." The man hopped into the back seat. Preston jumped in the driver's seat with Mike riding shotgun. They peeled out in pursuit of the Mercedes, which they could see in the distance. Both cars sped down the river road. They watched Cue turn sharply left, almost spinning off the road, onto the Pont de la Concorde.

"Well, that's a break." Preston watched them turn left onto the bridge. "They can't go too fast through the busy section of Paris." Preston, noticing a jar of bloody Mary mix in the front seat, concluded their passenger had already had a few.

"Forward ho, brothers! My name's Ernie." Ernie held his drink up in a toast. "Wait till I tell my army buddies about this when I get back from leave."

Preston and Mike remained focused on the blue Mercedes in front of them. "Can't figure out why they would head this way," Mike said. "I would have thought they would flee Paris."

"Cue's up to something," Preston answered. "Looks like all the smoke has dissipated. Maybe we'll see a police car around here."

They continued to follow cue, but were not able to get closer, both cars moved swiftly down the Boulevard Raspail. "Hey, brothers, did you guys see the fires all over the city?' Ernie shook his head. "I thought the Russians had attacked. Scared the hell out of me. Hey, if you want to ram that car, it's OK with me. You can't hurt this clunker. Solid as a tank."

"They're slowing down," Preston observed. "There's nothing around here but the Catacombs."

"What's that?" Mike asked.

"An underground cemetery where the bones of millions of ex-Parisians are buried—a narrow, mazelike series of tunnels." Preston watched the Mercedes jump the curb and smash into the entrance to the tourist section of the Catacombs, shattering the door into pieces. Cue and Bela exited the car and dashed through the open entrance, while Preston pulled up to the side of the Mercedes.

"Let's roll, Mike," Preston urged. "We can't lose sight of them or we'll never catch up to them." He pitched a one-hundred dollar bill at Ernie. "Thanks for the loan of the car. See if you can flag down a French policeman." The two ran through the entrance.

"Good luck, mu brothers," Ernie yelled. Meanwhile, the scared Japanese tourist climbed over the trunk and frantically rushed down the sidewalk, screaming for help.

Preston and Mike, in close pursuit, descended the steps until they reached the bottom floor, where they saw words carved into the mortared stone wall: STOP—HERE IS THE EMPIRE OF DEATH.

"Well, that's nice," Mike mumbled as they ran down the dimly lit passageway. On each side there were neatly organized bones, laid into stacks and geometric designs. One wall consisted entirely of skulls, stacked from bottom to top. They couldn't see in the dimly lit tunnel, but they could hear footsteps. Their chase continued down the damp, cold passageway.

Preston heard the sound of an iron gate being kicked open. "Just as I figured. They're entering the tunnels that have been off limits for nearly two centuries." They continued their chase down one narrow tunnel, then another, still not being able to see clearly. They heard rats scurrying and squealing as they darted past.

"Preston, I can see them ahead." Mike pointed his gun.

"Cue has got to be out of breath by now, damn it," Preston complained. "I sure as hell am."

"Look out!" Bela stopped and turned around. "Hit the dirt."

Both returned fire and dove spread eagle on the floor as Bela fired off several shots. The dark silhouette figure fell to the floor.

"We got him!" Preston hollered.

"He got me, too." Mike answered. Preston reached down to pick Mike up. "The son of a bitch shot my gun right out of my hand," Mike groaned. "And the bullet ricocheted into my right thigh." Mike sighed. "But hell, it could have been worse. If he hadn't hit my gun, the bullet would have ripped through my chest."

"You need to retreat back and get some medical attention," Preston urged.

"I'll be all right. I'll use my undershirt for a tourniquet; it's not that bad a wound. Go find Cue before you lose him."

"Hope to see you around, Mike." Preston raced down

the narrow passageway. The ceiling's dim lights grew farther and farther apart. He approached Bela, who lay sprawled on the floor. Preston picked up the man's gun.

"Good riddance, ol' boy," he said. "I'm sure your father will be glad to see you. Cue, you fat bastard, there's no way you can keep this chase going." He grew more cautious now; Cue could be waiting for him almost anywhere. Preston slowed his pace, looking carefully ahead.

No sign of Cue. Just piles and piles of skeletons. "Surely he didn't go down that side passage. It could be a dead end.

Suddenly from behind, he heard Cue's voice: "Stop right there, Preston." Cue had been hiding in a narrow crevasse. "Pitch both guns down the tunnel." Cue motioned at him with his gun. "Now get on your knees and lean against that pile of skeletons."

Preston did what he was told, leaning against a tall stack of bones. Cue, still breathing heavily, pointed his gun directly at Preston. "You've meddled in my affairs for the last time. You've wrecked my dreams of adding *Mona Lisa* to my collection. Preston remained quiet and completely still. "Now I'm forced to have my security guards load up my paintings and other antiques and leave the castle tomorrow. But there will be countless treasures that I will never see again. At least I'll have permanent refuge. No one will ever know where I am—ever."

Preston broke in: "Mike has sought reinforcements. These tunnels will soon be swarming with French authorities. All they can get you for is breaking and entering. Come to your senses—you don't want to be charged for first degree murder."

"Good try," spat Cue. "But I know a back passageway that will take me far, far away from where we are now, and soon I'll be on my merry way to Chamonix." Cue stared at Preston with immense hatred.

"Good bye, Preston. Pleasant dreams." Cue aimed his gun straight at Preston's heart. In a last ditch effort, Preston grabbed a splintered skeleton rib bone and lunged at Cue. But it was not in time. Cue pulled the trigger.

There was just a click. He pulled the trigger again. Another click.

"Damn," Cue moaned.

Preston approached the retreating Cue. "There's a pool term for that. You scratched."

"There's always another game," Cue retorted. He reached into his vest pocket and pulled out a small derringer.

Preston lunged forward, grabbing Cue's hand, but it was too late—Cue was able to fire off the shot. The bullet ripped through Preston's left side, just below his left shoulder. Preston jabbed the splintered rib bone into Cue's neck, piercing his jugular. Blood splurted out. Cue fell back against the mortared stone wall, his eyes glazed.

"Sorry about that, Fatso. Where you're going, there aren't going to be any smiling *Mona Lisa*s or beautiful maidens frolicking." Preston smirked. "Just ugly, toothless women with horns and pitchforks. Hope you enjoy." He started to walk away, then stopped and faced Cue. "Oh, I almost forgot. Pleasant dreams." Preston picked up his gun and dog trotted back toward the front entrance. His wound was minor, but he was bleeding and didn't have anything to slow the blood flow. "Stupid jumpsuit," he muttered. "Hope I can find the damn entrance in this maze." Then he heard a loud whistle blowing, down the dimly lit tunnel.

"Preston," a man with a French accent hollered. "Preston James, can you hear me?" Preston shouted as loud as his lungs would let him: "Damn right, I hear you. Keep coming down the passageway!" Minutes later, the men met. Preston was glad to see the French police uniform.

"Preston, I'm Jean-Paul LeJuene. Are you OK?"

"Damn glad to see you." Preston shook the man's hand. "I've been hit, but it's not bad."

Jean-Paul unzipped Preston's jumpsuit and pulled it off his shoulders. "I brought a first aid kit with me, just in case you needed it. Apparently it was a good idea." Jean-Paul cleaned the wound, treated it and wrapped bandages tightly around his upper chest. "That will work until we can get you to a hospital. We've been looking for you.

"Is my fellow agent, Mike, OK?"

"Yes, we took him to the hospital. He'll be all right."

"What about Sabrina?" Preston inquired, "The woman who was tied up in the Louvre?"

"That I don't know. But we have men all over the museum."

"Please, *please* tell me you have a cigarette for me."

"Why, yes I do." Jean-Paul pulled out a pack and handed one to Preston, lighting it.

"God bless you." Preston took several deep drags. "Let's get the hell out of this skeleton graveyard, before Bela Lugosi shows up."

"Who?"

"Never mind, it's not important."

Suddenly, out of a narrow side tunnel, Cue appeared, his blood-soaked undershirt wrapped around his neck. He approached Preston from behind, staggering forward, barely able to stand. He lunged at Preston's neck, holding the splintered bloody rib bone.

"Preston, look out!" Jean-Paul reached for his gun.

Preston turned just in time to grab Cue's arm. The rib bone dropped from his hand. He jerked the bloody t-shirt off Cue's neck and slapped it across his face, pushing him backward. Cue fell face-down on the floor.

"You want my gun?"

"Not necessary. This was his final hurrah."

"Let's get you out of here," Jean-Paul said. "I want to warn you, news travels fast in Paris. There will be gawking tourists, locals, TV crews, you name it."

"After what all I have gone through the last several days"—Preston smiled—"it will be the least of my worries."

Four hours later at the American Hospital in Paris, a pretty young nurse led Colonel Randolph down the second floor hallway. "Your agents are in this room," the nurse said. "Mr. James has been sedated and is probably still asleep, but Mr. O'Grady is quite restless, and is ready to leave."

The colonel entered the room, "Hello, Mike," the Colonel said. "You doing okay?"

"They got me in the leg," Mike answered.

"How's Preston?'

"He has a minor wound beneath his shoulder," Mike reported. "He's exhausted—he's been asleep for going on three hours."

"Not asleep anymore." Preston stood up. "Colonel, nice of you to stop by."

"You know I hate to give compliments"—the Colonel

smiled—"but I must say both of you did one hell of a job."

"And what about me?" Sabrina entered the room and took Preston's hand. "I came by twice earlier, but I didn't want to awake you."

"Are you all right?" Preston asked. "I was worried Bela had broken your neck."

"I'm okay." Sabrina grinned. "I have a nice bruise on the back of my neck, and I'm a little worn out."

"You're lucky Sebastian wanted Bernard to do his dirty work."

Sabrina and the Colonel pulled up chairs in between the two beds.

"I want to hear everything that happened, from when you did your trapeze act over to Cue's balcony until your adventures ended in the Catacombs," the Colonel said. "But you can tell me all about it tomorrow at breakfast, over mimosas. As of today, by the way, eight British intelligent agents, fifteen Swiss agents, and three of our men are either at Cue's castle or are on their way. Also, we've notified several art historians, who'll identify and return the oil paintings, antiques, and heirlooms to their rightful owners."

"What about my belongings?" Sabrina asked.

"Already taken care of. They're sent air freight to Preston's flat in London sometime today.

"Thank you for taking care of that," Sabrina said. "I appreciate your secretary, Danielle. She found out my sizes, and neatly packed several outfits, makeup, toilet articles, and other sundries into a suitcase I found in my room."

The Colonel added, "Danielle is also bringing a couple of wardrobe changes and toiletries for you, Preston. Both of you will be taken care of until you travel back to London tomorrow on the two o'clock flight."

"By the way, Preston, I meant to ask you earlier," Mike said, "where the hell did you get that ridiculous jumpsuit?"

"We'll talk about that tomorrow, Mike. But we're not going to wait until tomorrow to know how you happened to show up at the Louvre."

"Well," Mike began, "you can thank Cue's butler, Barrymore, who has a crush on Sabrina. When they left for their trip to Paris, Barrymore called the Swiss authorities and informed them of what was about to happen. They didn't believe him—thought it was a prank phone call. Fortunately, our commander here had asked the top brass of Swiss Intelligence to notify him at once if they heard anything about Cue's activities. The Colonel was notified of Cue's supposed plans, but not until deep into the night.

The Colonel interjected, "I was at a hotel in Chartres, tailing a suspected Russian agent, when I got the call from Danielle. I called Mike and informed him of what Barrymore had told the Swiss authorities, told him to get over to the Louvre immediately. I also called the French authorities, and told them what was going to happen at around seven o'clock at the Louvre. They were skeptical, but they managed to show up"—the Colonel displayed his disgust—"thirty minutes late."

"Anyway," Mike continued, "I got there around 6:30 and hid in a row of hedges not far from the Pyramid. I watched the van and Cue's Mercedes pull up, but I couldn't take all four of them on in the open—that would risk killing both of you in the crossfire. I waited until they entered the Pyramid and followed."

"All right, everyone," the Colonel broke in. "We'll meet tomorrow at nine for breakfast at the Café de Flore."

"Sabrina, I suggest you return to your room," said Preston, "and take a long nap. I'll come down and get you about seven tonight, and we'll take a taxi over to the Tour D'Argent restaurant. Have you ever been there?"

"Heard of it," Sabrina answered, "but never been."

"You'll love it. It's one of the most celebrated eating places in all of Paris. Overlooks the Seine, with a superb view of Notre Dame in the background."

"Sounds exciting." Sabrina waved goodbye and headed down the hallway.

"Mike, you want to join us? You're more than

welcome."

"Going to have to pass. They want me to stay overnight, to make sure I'm free of infections."

Preston smiled. "This is a first: leaving one hospital room to pick up my date in another hospital room.

"What a view," Sabrina said as she sat at the corner table, looking out the huge plate glass windows. They were high above the Seine River. Notre Dame Cathedral glowed across the river.

"That's why they call Paris the City of Light. There's no other city as magical and majestic."

The two ordered Dom Pérignon and discussed what had transpired over the last few days.

"Well," Preston asked, "where do we go from here?"

"I don't know." Sabrina smiled. "Where *do* we go from here?"

"I know one thing. I'm retiring from the espionage business. I've had enough."

"Good decision. Considering you're a cat that has used up his nine lives—and then some. I've had enough, too. I'm resigning from the CIA, effective tomorrow."

"Then what?" Preston asked

"I wouldn't mind working for the Colonel, if—and

only if—I were involved in tracking down art heists. I think that would be a nice challenge, and a safe one, too."

"I agree," Preston said. "We will propose it to the Colonel tomorrow and see what he has to say. If nothing else, it would provide a nice cover for his organization. Where are we going to reside?"

"We?" Sabrina smiled. "You got a mouse in your pocket?' Preston smiled, but didn't answer. "How about six months in Paris and six months in London?"

"Sounds like a winner to me."

"But I must inform you, I want to become a mother in the near future. One child is all I want. You have a problem with that?"

"Absolutely not."

"Then again," Sabrina said with a shy smile, "I don't want our child to be illegitimate."

"Neither do I."

"Well." Sabrina took a slow sip from her champagne glass, smiled, and waited.

"Sabrina, I love you." Preston held his glass up for a toast.

"I love you too, Preston. Very much."

"Will you marry me?' Preston quietly asked.

"Of course I will." Preston leaned across and kissed her softly on the lips.

"I say we take thirty days off, take a Mediterranean cruise around the Greek islands and Italy, and then rent a car and travel through Italy. We'll find an old church to get married in."

"Sounds like music to my ears." Sabrina's face flushed with excitement. "I'm ready anytime." Preston lit up two cigarettes and handed one to Sabrina. "Promise me that after we finish our trip, we'll put away these for good?'

"Word of honor," Preston said. "I've always said that when I retired from the espionage business, I would quit these damn things."

"By the way, if we have a boy we are not going to name his Preston James II. You got a problem with that?"

"I totally agree," Preston answered, "how about naming him Sebastian?"

"Funny little boy, aren't you?"

"I say we take a taxi to the café where we met on the Champs-Elysees, and share a bottle of Dom Pérignon."

"Well," Sabrina smiled, "what are we waiting for?"

Dr. Cue